DUPLICITY

A compelling Scottish murder mystery

PETE BRASSETT

THE
BOOK
FOLKS

Paperback published by The Book Folks

London, 2017

ISBN 978-1-5212-5804-0

www.thebookfolks.com

For John Hill.
Thank you for being miserable.

DUPLICITY is the fourth novel by Pete Brassett to feature detectives Munro and West. Look out for the preceding titles, SHE, AVARICE, and ENMITY, and TERMINUS and TALION which follow this one. All of these books can be enjoyed on their own, or as a series.

Chapter 1

Angus pulled up outside the house – an undeniably quaint sandstone cottage with a rambling front lawn bounded by a picket fence – nodded in the direction of the mustard-yellow Porsche Carrera parked outside, turned to his wife and winked. She shook her head, glowered disapprovingly and stepped from the car. Had it been something a little more discreet, something a little less ostentatious, then her opinion of the Carduccis may have been tempered but Italians were not renowned for their conservatism.

Heather Buchanan was not given to bouts of jealousy but even after twenty-two years the second Sunday of each month still managed to raise her hackles. Unlike her own house which was completely devoid of clutter and regularly scrubbed to within an inch of its life, the Carducci's home, with a plethora of empty wine glasses about the lounge, half-read newspapers strewn across the sofa and a cobweb or two hanging from the light fittings was, by comparison, positively unkempt.

Dining with Remo and Anita was a tradition as reliable as Christmas and one which invariably ended in an evening of bacchanalian proportions thanks largely to Remo's well-stocked wine cellar and Angus's complete inability to look a Barolo in the eye and say "no". Dreading the culinary marathon they referred to simply as "lunch", Heather rang the bell and smiled politely as Remo, sporting his trademark polo shirt and beige chinos, answered the door, a welcoming grin smeared across his face.

'Dinnae stand there gawping,' he said enthusiastically, 'we've a Bardolino on the go, come get yourselves a glass.'

She handed him her coat and flinched as the pungent aroma of garlic and wild herbs assaulted her senses. Her rendition of a traditional roast – something she considered to be her signature dish – comprised a lump of meat incinerated to the point of oblivion, served with over-cooked vegetables and, if she could be bothered, perhaps a Yorkshire pudding or two, all of which could be consumed in less than twenty minutes. Anita's version, passed down from generation to generation, was traditional in the Italian sense and, much to Heather's annoyance, was more a test of endurance than a meal. There was always a first course, *the antipasto*, then *il primo*, then the main, and finally the *dolce* followed by several hours spent quaffing yet more wine on the sofa as Angus and Remo regaled stories of their not-quite-legal shenanigans as young stevedores toiling away at the Port of Troon.

Angus, having forsaken breakfast in anticipation of the impending gastronomic delight, brushed excitedly past his wife, slapped Remo on the shoulder and scurried impatiently to the kitchen where Anita, threatening to spill from her figure-hugging dress, was laying the table with platters of salami, prosciutto, mortadella, provolone and fontina, a large bowl of mixed olives and a jug stuffed with sticks of grissini.

'That looks terrific!' he said, grinning boyishly as he ogled her décolletage.

Anita popped an olive seductively into her mouth and tucked a tress of jet black hair behind her ear.

'You'd not be saying that if Heather was behind you,' she said, smiling as she handed him a glass of wine.

'I was referring to the spread!'

'Of course you were.'

'All I'm saying is, it's a feast for the eyes. And the food's not bad either!'

'You're incorrigible. So, where is Heather?'

'Probably wilting under the gaze of your husband, I imagine,' said Angus. 'More importantly, what utterly delectable delight are you serving up today?'

'Arrosto d'Agnello all'Arezzo,' said Anita, with an exaggerated flourish of the hands.

'I was hoping you'd say that. What is it?'

'Leg of lamb with garlic, rosemary and lemon.'

'Great, can't wait to see the look on Heather's face.'

'Fond of her lamb, is she?'

'Aye, but she's not so keen on the garlic!'

Heather, face flushed, sauntered into the kitchen with Remo in tow, his hands gently gripping her shoulders as though he were steering a scooter.

'It's awful warm in here,' she said, 'is it me, Anita, or do you have the heat on?'

'It's you hen,' said Angus, smiling mischievously, 'you're suffering from what they call acute Remo-i-tis, you should know by now the old Latin temperament is closer to boiling point than your own. If you're not careful you'll end up with third degree burns.'

'He's not wrong,' said Anita, laughing, 'I get a heat rash at least three times a week.'

Heather, embarrassed by the smutty juvenile japes, slipped silently into a chair and, sipping timidly from a glass of fizzy water, enviously eyed the feast before her, glancing up only occasionally to scowl at her husband as he continued with the innuendo-laden banter.

By the time dessert was served, Heather, having conceded somewhat begrudgingly that the *linguine marina* and the roast lamb was nothing less than perfection on a plate, could abstain no longer and willingly accepted a chilled glass of Limoncello which, much to Angus's amusement, she knocked back like a shot of tequila before requesting a refill, giggling as the intoxicating lemon liqueur numbed her senses.

'Take it easy, doll,' said Remo, smirking, 'if you carry on like that, I'll have to carry you home!'

'In your dreams, Remo Carducci. No, no. Taxi's booked for nine o'clock as normal.'

'Good. Hey, Angus, I was thinking, just yesterday as it happens, do you recall…'

'Here we go,' said Anita, 'is it that time already?'

'…do you recall that numpty who came at us with a crowbar one time?'

'No, you've lost me there,' said Angus, 'oh, aye, hold on, I do. Crawford was his name. Why did he come after us?'

'You mean you can't remember? Dear God, is your memory going? The watches!'

Angus frowned as he stared pensively into space before laughing out loud.

'The watches! Of course!'

'Come on then,' said Anita, 'what's all this about the watches?'

'See here, hen,' said Remo, smiling as he reminisced, 'this Crawford fella, he was minted, right? Silver spoon and all that, always wore a suit. Anyways, he used to come all the way from Stirling to see if we had anything he could sell on for a profit.'

'Hold on,' said Heather, 'what you really mean is that he came to see what you'd managed to accidentally off-load from the ship without anyone noticing.'

'Aye, if you like. Anyway, as it happens we'd a boat in from Sweden and a part of her cargo was from a jeweller, and a part of the jeweller's shipment was a wee crate of watches. Halda, if I remember correctly.'

'That's right!' said Angus, 'I remember! Worth a wee fortune they were. So we said we'd *procure* them for him. For a substantial fee, naturally.'

'And was it?' said Anita. 'Substantial?'

'Enough to buy my first car,' said Angus. 'Morris Minor. Second-hand.'

'So, what happened?' said Heather, 'I mean, why the crowbar?'

'Well,' said Remo, 'we'd already taken his cash and arranged to meet him on the harbour road to hand over the goods when we had, shall we say, a better offer. So we took that deal instead.'

'So, this fellow from Stirling, this Crawford chappie, he came at you because, what? Because you'd reneged on the deal after you'd taken his money?'

'No, no, we didnae renege on anything,' said Remo. 'we just supplied him with some *alternative* merchandise.'

'Alternative merchandise?' said Anita, smiling. 'And I wonder what that could've been, then?'

'Rollmops. Two hundred jars of pickled herring!'

'He wasnae happy, I can tell you!' said Angus, laughing. 'He was that mad, he came back a few hours later, crowbar in one hand and a wheel-brace in the other looking to skelp the pair of us.'

'What did you do?'

'What could we do?' said Remo. 'We couldnae call the police now, could we? I mean, he was in the wrong and we were in the wrong. It was a dispute that had to be settled without the involvement of third parties.'

'So come on,' said Anita, 'dinnae keep us in suspense. What happened?'

'Well,' said Angus, lowering his voice, 'we didnae fancy losing our jobs or spending a week or two in the infirmary for that matter, so quick-thinking Remo here took the fellow to one side and asked him if he'd ever heard of the Carducci family. The Carduccis from Sicily.

The Carduccis who had a habit of making people disappear!'

'You never did!'

'Aye, right enough. Never saw him again.'

'Which reminds me,' said Remo, 'of the fella who did buy the watches, you'll not believe what happened to him but, before we go on, it's time we opened another bottle, I'll just…'

'No, no,' said Angus, checking his watch, 'hold on, I forgot, we've a treat for you. I've left it in the car.'

'A treat? And what would that be, then?'

'Amarone. A 2007 Amarone Riserva.'

'Thanking you!'

'Be right back.'

'You know something, Heather,' said Anita as Angus nipped outside, 'if it wasn't for us, these two would still be on the look-out for anything off the back of a lorry.'

'Oh, I'm not so sure. Angus perhaps, at least you two had the family business to fall back on.'

'Maybe,' said Remo, 'but there's only so much you can make from selling fish suppers six nights a week.'

'And the cafés.'

'Oh aye. Fair point. We've Angus to thank for that. His idea.'

'Well, you make a good team so well done you but it doesn't mean to say you dinnae need a good woman to keep you on the straight and narrow.'

'Is that so?' said Remo, 'Like the two of you never did anything a wee bit wrong?'

'Never,' said Heather, 'well, not recently anyway. Besides, the worst I ever did was sneaking into the pictures without paying.'

'So you're not in the same league as my beautiful wife, then?'

'What do you mean?' said Anita, smirking.

'Where shall I start? How about the fags and the booze you used to sell at school? I'll not mention where you got it from. And then there's the make-up you could never afford but always had, and let's not forget…'

'Och, that was years ago, Remo. Ancient history. Besides, we were all at it.'

'Aye, right enough, all I'm saying is: people in glass houses, etcetera. Now, what's keeping Angus, is he treading the grapes himself?'

'I'll go see,' said Heather, 'daft beggar's probably fallen over and split his head open, if we're lucky.'

Remo gave his wife a playful pat on the rump, grabbed the corkscrew and four clean glasses from the cupboard and headed for the lounge only to be greeted by an ashen-faced Heather standing motionless in the doorway.

'What is it, hen?' he said. 'Are you okay? You look like you've seen a ghost.'

Heather stared back, open-mouthed, her lips quivering.

'I… I'm not sure.'

'Heather?' said Anita, concerned. 'What's wrong? Where's Angus?'

'I don't know. He's… he's gone.'

Chapter 2

DC Dougal McCrae was a past master at drawing the short straw. Sunday afternoons were made for relaxing which, for most people, involved following a leisurely pursuit like a trip to the cinema or, so far as he was concerned, spending a few uninterrupted hours in tranquil bliss on the banks of a loch, rod in hand, waiting for the trout to bite – not packing up early and travelling all the way to Kirkmichael, pleasant as it was, to investigate a missing person.

He drove to the end of Straiton Road, parked his scooter behind the two squad cars straddling the verge and watched as a couple of officers conducted a door-to-door along the deserted street while three more trudged, somewhat begrudgingly, through the meadow opposite the Carducci's house.

'Hello?' he said, trying not to sound disgruntled as he rapped the front door, 'Is there anybody home?'

Remo appeared, a look of consternation on his face.

'Can I help?'

'DC McCrae,' said Dougal, flashing his warrant card, 'mind if I come in?'

Heather, clutching a small glass of brandy, sat huddled next to Anita on the sofa, her angst-ridden face pale and drawn.

'This here fella's a detective,' said Remo as he ushered him into the lounge, 'he's come to… well, detect I suppose.'

'I'm sorry,' said Heather, 'for all the fuss and bother. I know you're meant to wait twenty-four hours before reporting…'

'No, no,' said Dougal with a reassuring smile, 'that's a fallacy, madam. If you're concerned about the welfare of somebody, anybody, you can call us as just soon as you like. And you must be?'

'Heather Buchanan.'

'And it's your husband that's gone missing?'

'Aye. Angus. That's right.'

'And you, Sir?'

'Remo Carducci and that's my wife Anita. Heather and Angus were joining us for lunch. We've already told the police out there what happened.'

'I appreciate that, Sir,' said Dougal, 'but I'm led to believe the circumstances surrounding his disappearance are quite unusual, that's why I've been asked to look into it. So, if you dinnae mind, would you run over it again for my benefit, just so's I can get things straight in my own head?'

'Of course,' said Anita, smoothing down her dress as she stood, 'but you'll be needing a cup of tea, Constable…?'

'Detective Constable McCrae, madam. Thanks very much. So, why don't you tell me what happened.'

'Not much to tell,' said Remo, 'it's all just a wee bit, well, odd. We'd finished lunch see and I was about to open some more wine when Angus said he'd a bottle in the car, so he went to fetch it.'

'And what time was this?'

'About three-thirty I reckon or thereabouts.'

'So he went to fetch the wine and…?'

'And that's it. He just disappeared. We got tired of waiting for him to come back, it wasn't long, five minutes maybe, that's all, but he was only going to the car so Heather here stepped outside to see what was keeping him and he was gone. Vanished.'

'I see,' said Dougal, 'and you've looked about the place? I mean, he'd not nipped back inside? To use the bathroom, maybe?'

'No, no,' said Heather, 'we've searched the whole house from top to bottom and we've been up and down the street a half a dozen times and Remo's even driven back to my home to see if he was there but it's all locked up, just as we left it.'

'Have you tried calling him? I'm assuming he has a mobile?'

'He has,' said Heather, 'and it's in his coat pocket. And his coat's hanging in the hall. See here, Mr McCrae, that's what's so odd. The only thing he took with him was the car key and the car's still locked and the bottle of wine's still on the back seat. He didnae even close the front door when he went out.'

Dougal sat next to Heather as Anita returned carrying a steaming mug and a small plate of biscuits.

'Sorry,' she said, 'just a teabag, hope that's okay.'

'That's perfect, Mrs Carducci. Thank you. Tell me, have you any idea where your husband may have gone? I mean, I know his departure was unexpected but, for example, does he smoke? Could he have nipped to the pub to get a packet of fags, maybe?'

'The pub's a thirty second walk up the street, Detective,' said Remo, 'not a three-hour hike. And no, apart from a panatella at Christmas, he doesn't smoke.'

'Fair enough. And I take it that, apart from yourselves, there's no-one else hereabouts he might have called on?'

'No,' said Heather, 'Remo and Anita are the only folk we know in the village.'

'So, you can't think of a single reason why he may have left so abruptly?'

'Mr McCrae,' said Heather indignantly, 'if there's one thing my Angus looks forward to every month it's lunch with Sophia bloody Loren here, sorry Anita, I didn't mean… anyways, he'd not give that up for anything.'

Anita sat next to Heather, took her hand and smiled warmly.

'We've known each other for decades, Constable,' she said, 'we're like brothers and sisters. There's just no way Angus would up and leave without saying something, it's simply not in his nature.'

'Okay,' said Dougal, draining his mug, 'I have to admit, as you say, it's all a wee bit odd, folk dinnae just disappear into thin air so here's what we'll do. I'll have a word with the officers outside just now and see what's happening. It'll be dark in a couple of hours so we'll have to organise another search of the area for tomorrow. Mr Carducci, if you're not averse to the suggestion, I'd like you to stay here in case he comes back. Mrs Carducci, perhaps you could stay with Mrs Buchanan at her house tonight? I'm sure you'll not want to be alone, am I right, Heather?'

'Right enough. Thank you. Would you mind Anita? I wouldnae want to put you to any trouble.'

'It's no trouble, hen. I'll just grab a few bits and bobs and we'll be on our way.'

'Good. I'll get one of the cars out front to drop you round,' said Dougal, 'one more thing before I go: can you let me have a recent photo of your husband? and I'll need some personal details too – age, what he was wearing, that kind of thing and, if you dinnae mind, I'd like his bank details, too.'

'Bank details?' said Heather. 'Why on earth…?'

'See here, Mrs Buchanan, when folk go missing, chances are they'll not get far without some cash in their pocket. Tracking their bank account for signs of activity is one of the best ways of keeping tabs on them. It also reassures us that they're still… that nothing untoward has happened to them.'

'That's very clever, Mr McCrae. His wallet's in his coat, I'll fetch his bank card for you now. When would you need the photo?'

'Just as soon as. I'll drop by your house tomorrow morning if that's okay? Then we'll get a few wee posters about the place, too. It's a tiny village. Someone, somewhere, must've seen something.'

Chapter 3

DI Munro, hands clasped behind his back, stood on the balcony of the second floor flat and contemplated the view towards the Firth of Clyde, smiling ruefully as he recalled the sight of trawlers chugging home along the Ayr flanked by flocks of gulls squawking and swooping as they dived for titbits, a memory which, with the demise of the fishing industry, was rooted in the all too distant past. West dumped the rucksack containing all her worldly goods in the bedroom, joined him outside and took a lungful of fresh, sea air.

'Alright, Jimbo?' she said, smiling.

Munro, lost in thought, stared dead ahead.

'You know something, Charlie?' he said with a wistful sigh. 'I used to come here as a wean, not to fish like, just to watch the boats. I'd sit down there on the harbour wall and just watch. There used to be all sorts coming and going back then, not just the trawlers mind, there were ships from all over. I'd watch them and I'd say to myself: when I grow up, I'm going to be like Para Handy, piloting a puffer laden with coal or timber, battling against the elements on my way to Arran and Jura and Mull and Skye.

In charge of my own destiny but at the mercy of the waves.'

'A typical "Boy's Own" adventure, eh?' said West. 'So how come you didn't follow your dream?'

'Cannae swim. One hit from a twelve-footer and I'd have been on my way to Davy Jones's Locker.'

'Come on then,' said West, laughing, 'tell me what you think, does it pass muster?'

Munro turned around, leant against the railings and folded his arms as he surveyed the building. Mariner's Wharf, a relatively new complex built in a style reminiscent of a Victorian waterside warehouse was, he had to concede, aesthetically acceptable.

'Well,' he said, rubbing his chin, 'it's pleasant enough to look at...'

'Two bedrooms,' said West, interrupting, 'new kitchen, parking, away from the town centre so nice and quiet and don't forget the view, I mean, imagine what the sunsets must be like from here.'

'Are you selling it to me or trying convince yourself you've done the right thing?'

'The latter, I think. Anyway, it'll do for now. I can always move just as soon as I find myself a nice little cottage with a garden somewhere.'

'Good luck with that. Och, I'm joking you. Look, you'll be happy here, what's more you can walk to the office, it's not far at all.'

'Not sure if that's good or bad,' said West, 'still, doesn't bear thinking about, I'm not starting for a couple of days yet.'

'You'll be fine. Listen, it's not as if you're starting a new job where you dinnae know your arsenal from your Elgin. You're familiar with the place now and you'll be working with young Dougal again. He's a good lad.'

'Yeah, you're right I suppose. By the way, I never said thanks for the lift, for running me up here I mean. You didn't have to.'

'Nae bother lassie, you dinnae want to be fussing with public transport when you're moving into your new flat, it's a cause for celebration although I have to admit it'll not be the same without a drink or two.'

'Why's that?'

'I have to drive home!'

'Oh, yeah. Shame. What time do you have to go?'

'Och there's no rush, I've the whole day ahead.'

'Great! In that case, how about giving me a lift to the supermarket so I can stock up on stuff and then maybe we can go pick up my car?'

'I may be nearing retirement, Charlie, but I dinnae work for Uber. Not yet, anyway.'

* * *

Munro pulled over, waited for the traffic to pass and executed yet another U-turn as West, cursing, fumbled with her phone.

'Charlie,' he said, his patience fading, 'if you waste any more time with that blessed sat-nav of yours there's a fair chance we'll end up in Timbuktu and I'm not dressed for the climate. There's a map in the glove compartment, I take it you're old enough to remember what a map is?'

'Sadly, yes.'

'Do you actually have any idea at all where it is we're meant to be going?'

'Some place called Mauchline,' said West, desperately flicking through the pages, 'Fernlea Avenue. Ah, found it. Where are we now?'

'Good grief,' said Munro, shaking his head. 'We've just passed Tarbolton. For the second time, I might add.'

'Okay, okay. We're a bit off but it's not far. Keep going, we're almost there.'

'When exactly did you buy this motor car, anyway? I cannae recall you looking at one the last time we were up.'

'I didn't. Got it the day before yesterday, off the internet. Ad in AutoTrader.'

'Are you joking me? So you've not even seen it?'

'Don't be daft, of course I have,' said West, 'they had a picture of it on the website. Quite a few as it happens.'

'I didnae have you down as one of the more-money-than-sense-brigade, lassie. There's no telling what state the vehicle's in.'

'Relax,' said West, 'it's got a full service history, three owners, good runner.'

'Aye, well, I'm saying nothing,' said Munro. 'What did you get? Is it a Defender? I could see you in a Defender. Be ideal up here when the snow starts to fall.'

'Dream on, I may have more money than sense but I'm not loaded.'

'Well I hope it's not a wee sports car, that would never do. You need something solid, well-built, reliable.'

'What? Like this knackered old thing?'

'I'll have you know that this Peugeot, like it's owner, is far from knackered.'

'Okay,' said West with a smile, 'life in the old dog yet, eh?'

Munro turned in to Fernlea Avenue half expecting to see a row of grey, pebble-dashed terraces but was pleasantly surprised to be greeted by a tree-lined street full of large, detached houses with well-tended gardens and block-paved driveways.

'We appear to have left Scotia and landed in Hampstead,' he said with a grin.

'Up there on the right, I think,' said West.

Munro pulled up and killed the engine.

'Okay lassie, on you go. I'll wait here. I hope you're not disappointed.'

West scurried up the path, rang the bell and disappeared inside only to reappear minutes later followed by a trendy, young man who, with his skinny jeans, black-rimmed glasses and a beard like Rasputin, would've looked more at home in Shoreditch. Munro, intrigued, stepped from the car and watched intently as they went to the garage, his initial surprise at the throaty roar of a turbocharged engine echoing off the walls turning to laughter as a car only Noddy would drive rolled sedately towards the street. West, beaming like a six-year-old at a birthday party, waved and beckoned him forward.

'I cannae believe it,' he said, doing his best to hide his amusement, 'you've bought yourself a beige pedal car.'

The beardy man laughed, handed over the keys and went inside.

'It's a Nissan Figaro,' said West, defensively, 'and for your information not only is it cool but it'll do a ton flat out.'

'I'll take your word for it.'

'And by the way, it's not beige, it's Topaz Mist.'

'Topaz Mist? I think I drank one of those in the pub last week. Are you not taking it for a wee test drive?'

'Nah, it'll be fine. Anything goes wrong, I know where he lives, right? Come on, race you back. Oh, hold on.'

West pulled her phone from her pocket and glanced at Munro, a worrying frown creased her face.

'DCI Elliot,' she said, 'what on earth could he want?'

'Well he's not calling to ask if you'd like some flowers on your desk. Answer it.'

'Sir?' said West, cautiously. 'How's it going?'

'Charlie! Glad I caught you,' said Elliot, 'listen, are you still down in Carsethorn?'

'No, I'm here in Ayr, been moving in to my new flat. Jimbo, I mean DI Munro, gave me a lift up.'

'James? Is he there with you?'

'Yup, standing right here.'

'Excellent. Listen, Charlie, I dinnae mean to impose but any chance you could drop by this afternoon? Something I'd like you to take a look at.'

'Well I'm not due to start for a couple of days yet, Sir, and I've just picked up my new car and I've got my flat to sort out, and…'

'Thanks Charlie, I knew I could count on you. Oh, and bring James, would you?'

West put the phone away, looked at Munro and shrugged her shoulders.

'He wants us to drop by,' she said, 'this afternoon.'

'Us?'

'That's what he said.'

'I dinnae like the sound of this, Charlie. I dinnae like the sound of this at all.'

Chapter 4

Dougal, having risen at dawn to call on the Carduccis, then coordinate an extended search of Kirkmichael and then conduct further enquiries regarding the disappearance of Angus Buchanan was, due to a lack of sleep, breakfast and coffee, not his normal ebullient self. His mood was buoyed, however, by the premature and wholly unexpected sight of DS West marching purposefully through the door with Munro trailing in her wake.

'Miss! Am I glad to see you!' he said, beaming broadly. 'You too, Boss, and not before time, I can tell you.'

'Someone's a happy puppy,' said West, perching on the edge of a desk.

'Quite the opposite,' said Dougal, 'I'm fizzing. What are you doing here anyway?'

'No idea. DCI Elliot asked us to drop by.'

'The Chief? Oh, I hope it's to lend a hand, I cannae do everything myself.'

'Well I'm not starting for a day or two yet, so I doubt it. Probably a pep talk or something I imagine.'

'How about you, Boss? Tell me you're here for the duration.'

'No, no,' said Munro with a smile, 'I hate to disappoint you, Dougal, but I'm just dropping my fare off.'

'Sorry?'

'Ignore me. So, where is George? I do hope he's not languishing in a bar some place.'

'He's right behind you, Boss,' said Dougal, raising a hand and pointing towards the door.

DCI Elliot, sleeves rolled up and grinning like a grizzly after a salmon supper, stepped forward and grabbed Munro by the hand.

'I've been looking forward to this,' he said, 'I appreciate you coming. How have you been James? Charlie?'

'Och, can't complain, George,' said Munro, 'it's not long now until I can finally put my feet up for good.'

'You'll be bored in no time, "feet up" is not in your nature, James. How about you Charlie? How's the flat?'

'Nice, thanks for asking,' said West, 'great view but I can't hang around too long, got stuff to sort, you know: cleaning, unpacking…'

'This'll not take long,' said Elliot. 'Here's the thing, I'm up to my ears see, trying to organise the roster but it's awful hard with so few men available. Problem I have is, I can't put a man on a case and then move him after a day or two, get what I'm saying?'

'Oh aye, right enough,' said Munro, 'you've got to have continuity.'

'Exactly. So look, Charlie, I know it's above and beyond the call of duty but we've had a missing persons filed. Dougal's been looking into it but it's not straightforward, he can fill you in and perhaps you can ponder it while you're getting yourself settled.'

'Alright,' said West, 'I'll try but no promises. I've still got quite a bit to do, including getting my bearings around town.'

'Och, James'll help you out, I'm sure. Isn't that right, James?'

'No, no,' said Munro, shaking his head as he surrendered his hands, 'that's me away just now. I've a drive ahead of me and hills to climb, plants to plant, and whisky to drink, so best of…'

'A couple of minutes, that's all,' said Elliot pleadingly, 'have a cup of tea while Dougal fills you in, eh? You're a man of experience, James, you could probably give these two a word of advice so they hit the ground running, so to speak.'

'I've a funny feeling the only place I'll be running to is home,' said West.

'Och, come then Dougal,' said Munro, rolling his eyes as he reluctantly unzipped his coat and pulled up a chair, 'let's have it, what's the story?'

* * *

Dougal plonked two mugs of tea on the desk as Elliot vacated the office, sat back and ruffled his hair, his cheeks puffing with a protracted, heavy sigh. Munro stared at the mug and the teabag bobbing on the surface.

'Are you okay, Dougal?' he said. 'Teabags? What happened to the pot?'

'Sorry, Boss, I cannae be arsed. I'm that tired, I havenae the patience nor the energy.'

'You look done in,' said West, 'been overdoing it?'

'No choice, Miss, I'm here on my own,' said Dougal. 'The Chief's got everyone else working on other things. He kept saying DS Cameron's replacement would be here soon enough but to be honest, I think he's been holding out for you.'

'I'll take that as a compliment. Have you had lunch?'

'No. No breakfast either, not unless Irn-Bru counts as one of my five a day.'

'Keep drinking that stuff, laddie, and the only five a day you'll be worrying about is the amount of teeth of you'll be losing,' said Munro. 'Okay, let's crack on then you can take yourself off and get something to eat.'

'Aye, okay. So, Angus Buchanan. Sixty-two years old, married to Heather, lives in Crosshill. Retired. Well, good as. Helps his business partner Remo Carducci run that chain of chippies and coffee shops.'

'Carducci's?' said Munro. 'The Italian cafes? Like the one in Irvine?'

'Aye, that's them. Irvine, Kilmarnock, Prestwick, Troon. There's one here too, down by the esplanade.'

'I've been to that one and I have to say the food was really quite excellent.'

West turned to face Munro with an inquisitive smirk on her face.

'You went to an Italian café?' she said. 'Did you actually have anything Italian to eat? I mean, proper Italian?'

'Aye, of course,' said Munro, 'I had 12oz bistecca lombata.'

'Thought so, you had a sirloin steak, with a generous helping of *patate fritte* no doubt. Go on, Dougal.'

'Miss. So, Angus Buchanan and his missus were having lunch with the Carduccis yesterday, they're old friends apparently…'

'And where was that?' said Munro.

'Kirkmichael, it's a tiny wee village not far from Crosshill and Maybole, bit of a one-horse town. Anyways, after lunch Mr Buchanan nipped out to his car to fetch a bottle of wine and never came back.'

'Doesn't sound too complicated to me,' said West, 'did they look for him? Probably drove off after an argument or something.'

'No, Miss,' said Dougal, 'here's the thing, he was only gone a couple of minutes when his wife went after him, there's absolutely no way he could've got far on foot in such a short space of time.'

'On foot?'

'Aye. His car wasnae touched. It was locked and the wine was still on the back seat. His wallet and his phone and his coat, all hanging up indoors.'

'So he just…?'

'Aye. Just disappeared. Vanished.'

'Maybe it's not us you should be talking to, Dougal,' said Munro with a grin, 'I suggest you contact Area 51.'

'Area 51?'

'Never mind. So, this Mr Buchanan, what's his medical history like?'

'Sorry?' said Dougal, frowning. 'Medical history?'

'Aye. Does he suffer from any ailments, depression or dementia maybe? Is he on any kind of medication? Has he a history of wandering off, perhaps?'

'Oh, I didnae think to ask.'

'Well stick it on the list and ask his wife. Last thing we want is someone on the loose without their tablets. So, apart from that, how far have you got?'

'I've logged him with the MPB and we've some posters to go up around the town tomorrow. We've also completed two searches of the area including door-to-doors but so far, absolutely nothing.'

'Any cameras about the place?' said West.

'None.'

'Anything else?'

'Apart from wanting to bash my head against a brick wall, you mean? No. Oh hold on, there is. I got his bank details so we can keep an eye on his account, see if he shows up somewhere.'

'Well done, laddie,' said Munro, 'good work.'

'Thanks, but I havenae got round to sorting it yet, not had time.'

Munro checked his watch and cast a sideways glance at West.

'Right,' he said, 'listen to me, Dougal. This is a one-off, never-to-be-repeated, very special offer, you understand? Give us the details and we'll sort it for you while you go get yourself some food.'

'Really? Thanks very much, Boss. Appreciate it.'

'There is one condition, mind.'

'Oh no,' said Dougal, 'what's that?'

'You get yourself something decent to eat, none of that pot-pourri chicken or raw fish that's causing havoc at the A&E, do I make myself clear?'

'Crystal. Here's his bank card, it's the Clydesdale. Alloway Street. Bottom of the High Street and keep going, it's on the way to the station.'

* * *

'Changed your mind?' said West as they made their way downstairs. 'About lending a hand, I mean?'

'No, no,' said Munro, laughing at the absurdity of the question, 'I'm not hanging around, lassie. The poor lad's overwhelmed so I'm simply doing him a favour, okay? You can consider it my deed for the day. My second deed of the day.'

'Second? What was the first?'

'Running you here, of course. Count yourself lucky I didnae switch the meter on.'

'You're all heart,' said West. 'Come on, we'll take my car, you can try it out.'

'Are you joking me? I'll not fit in that thing. No, no, until you get yourself a roof-rack so you can strap me on the top, we'll be travelling in mine for the foreseeable.'

* * *

Margaret McClure was, at sixty-years-old – forty-one of which had been spent at the Clydesdale – one of a dying breed. As manager of the Alloway Street branch, a position she'd held for nearly three decades, she employed an approach regarded by many, particularly those at head office, as old-fashioned and out of step with the times. Rather than concentrate on persecuting her customers with threats of legal action for exceeding their credit limits, she preferred to meet them face to face, to have a chat over a cup of tea to discuss their needs or alleviate their fears, to offer help and advice and to reassure them that the bank was their ally, not their foe. Unfortunately, the number of clients who actually visited the bank was dwindling at an alarming rate.

She loathed modern technology for facilitating the surge in online transactions thereby making the business of banking increasingly anonymous. She abhorred the way hard-working locals were granted or declined an overdraft based simply on their credit rating or postcode. But most of all she was saddened by the fact that she now saw less of her customers and more of her staff. She was simply biding her time, waiting for the axe to fall on her branch as the Clydesdale, like so many other banks, disappeared from the high street under the false claim that they were a drain on resources.

The fastidiously groomed brunette, dressed in a 1940s-style two-piece, stood and smiled politely, proffering her hand as Munro and West entered her office, grateful, if nothing else, for the company.

'Good afternoon, Inspector,' she said, her mood lifting as she caught sight of his steely, blue eyes, 'and Detective Sergeant West. Do come in, can I offer you some refreshment? Tea, coffee, or a glass of iced water, perhaps?'

'Very kind but no,' said Munro, entranced by her impeccable appearance, 'we'll not stay long. It's about a customer of yours.'

'Well fire away, Inspector. I'll certainly do my best to help.'

'Mr Angus Buchanan,' said West. 'Seems he's gone missing and we're concerned for his welfare so the first thing we'd like to do is keep an eye on his account. As you're no doubt aware, any sign of activity could prove vital in allowing us to locate him.'

'I quite understand, Sergeant, but you see, I can't do that here. I'm afraid that kind of action will have to be authorised by head office.'

'I appreciate that,' said West, sliding his bank card across the desk, 'but if you could get the ball rolling?'

'Of course. I'll see to it right away.'

'Thanking you,' said Munro, 'Now, Mrs McClure…'

'Miss.'

'Miss. Here's the thing. Mr Buchanan's been missing for a little over 24 hours now so in the meantime, while we wait for that to get sorted, would you mind taking a wee look on that computer of yours and letting us know if he's withdrawn any cash between now and say around 3pm yesterday?'

'Why certainly, Inspector,' said McClure, smiling demurely, 'although you know I can't divulge any details, not unless…'

'Aye, that's okay, we just need to know if…'

'Let me have a look for you.'

McClure's delicate fingers flew across the keyboard like tentacles sliding over a slippery rock.

'Here we are,' she said. 'Now, will it be just his current account you're interested in or the business account, too?'

'Business account?' said West. 'Didn't know he had one.'

'Oh yes. It's held in two names: Mr Buchanan and a Mr Carducci; they're both signatories.'

'I see,' said Munro, 'and are there any bank cards associated with that account, you know, for use in the cash machine?'

'No, cheque book only.'

'And there's not been any transfers or withdrawals or anything like that?'

'No, in fact by the looks of it hardly any money's come out of the account at all. The last debit was over a year ago and since then, just deposits.'

'Just deposits? Look, Miss McClure, I know you cannae go into specifics but does it have a healthy balance?'

'Inspector, I really can't…'

'All I'm asking is: is it healthy? A meal in a restaurant healthy? Two weeks in Florida healthy? Buy a new house healthy?'

McClure sat back and smiled at Munro.

'Not so much a new house, Inspector,' she said. 'More the entire street.'

'Are joking me? And is that account under their names or a business name?'

'It's a business name,' said McClure. 'Remus Trading.'

Munro coughed as if he had a large peanut lodged in the back of his throat.

'Did you say Rebus?'

'Remus.'

'Thank God for that.'

'I'd say it was an amalgamation of their Christian names: Remo and Angus.'

'Aye, right enough. Well if it's not too much trouble, would you mind asking the gentlemen at head office to keep an eye on that account too?'

'Of course, Inspector. Let me have your details and I shall make sure you're contacted should anything occur.'

* * *

'I spy,' said West with a mischievous smile as they walked back to the car, 'something beginning with "F".'

'What?'

'Something beginning with "F", go on.'

'Och, I'm not one for playing games Charlie,' said Munro, 'Financial institution?'

'Nope.'

'I give up.'

'Spoilsport.'

'Well come on, lassie,' said Munro, 'you cannae leave me hanging. What is it?'

'Foxy,' said West, grinning wildly.

'Foxy?'

'Foxy, flirty, frisky and fancy, as in, somebody fancies you!'

'Good grief.'

* * *

Dougal, having devoured his recommended daily dose of calories in a single sitting, smiled contentedly, wiped his mouth with a paper napkin and set about brewing a pot of tea just as Munro and West, her nose twitching at the scent of something appetising, returned to the office.

'Ah, Dougal,' she said, glancing at the empty box on the desk for any leftovers, 'you've got some colour back in your cheeks! Good lunch?'

'Aye, thanks Miss. I'm full to bursting now.'

'Not a bag of chips and a pickled egg, I hope?' said Munro.

'No, Boss. Pizza. Thin crust pepperoni, extra large.'

'Excellent! I'm glad to see you're embracing all things Italian because I've a wee something that may help with your inquiry, once you've poured a brew, that is.'

'Coming right up,' said Dougal, 'so what is it? Please tell me you know where he is.'

'I'm not a clairvoyant, laddie,' said Munro, as he took his tea and sat down. 'Companies House. See what you can find about an outfit called Remus Trading. Your Mr Buchanan and Signor Carducci have a business account by that name and it's in rude health, by which I mean, as rude as you can get without awarding it a triple-x rating.'

'Really? Okay, just give me a moment and I'll…'

'No, hold on, Dougal,' said Munro, frowning as he slowly placed his cup on the table, 'hold on. Remus. The name Remus. Remo and Angus, right?'

'That's what the bank manager said,' replied West, 'makes perfect sense. Why?'

'I've just had a thought. Romulus and Remus.'

'Oh aye,' said Dougal, 'the twins.'

'Sorry,' said West, 'haven't a clue what you're talking about. What twins?'

'Well, according to Roman mythology, Mars, the God of war had a whatsit with a lady called Rhea Silvia and they had twin boys: Romulus and Remus who are credited with building the city of Rome.'

'Gotcha,' said West, 'and Carducci's Italian so you're thinking maybe that's why they chose the name?'

'Exactly,' said Munro. 'There may be nothing in it but it's worth following up. Dougal, I suggest you have a chat with Carducci just as soon as you can, find out whereabouts in Italy he comes from and what exactly it is he and Mr Buchanan trade in. And let's hope he's no plans afoot to treat his partner the same way Romulus treated his brother.'

'What do you mean?' said West.

'He killed him. Charlie, go with Dougal, you need to meet Carducci, anyway.'

'Okey dokey.'

'Is that you away then, Boss?' said Dougal.

Munro glanced at his watch and sighed in a moment of rare indecisiveness.

'No. Look, I've an hour or so yet. I'll go see Buchanan's wife and get her side of the story. Incidentally, Dougal, did you speak to her about her husband's condition?'

'Aye, I did. Apparently he's as healthy as his bank account.'

Chapter 5

With little more than a primary school and a church, a post office and a general store, Crosshill – an old weaving village built by Irish immigrants – was regarded by the local community and visitors alike as quintessentially "sleepy". Driving past the whitewashed cottages lining a deserted Dalhowan Street, Munro, however, wondering if he'd missed the three-minute warning, considered it positively comatose.

Heather Buchanan, shrouded in a thick, woollen overcoat was incongruously conspicuous as she sat on an old spindle-back chair outside her house with the setting sun glinting off her glasses and a look of woeful abandonment on her face. Munro, not wishing to cause her alarm, stopped on the opposite side of the road and waved as he locked the car.

'Evening,' he said with a genial smile, 'Mrs Buchanan?'

'Aye,' said Heather, 'and who might you be?'

'James Munro. Detective Inspector James Munro. Retired. Well, trying to, anyway.'

'Trying?'

'I have a habit of getting… waylaid.'

'You mean you enjoy your work so much you dinnae want to leave?'

'Perhaps.'

'Or is it a fear of boredom? Not knowing what to do if you stop?'

'Probably.'

'I know how that feels, Inspector,' said Heather. 'I know how that feels. So, have you come to look for my husband?'

'Well, I'm going to try. Would you mind if I joined you?'

'Help yourself, you can fetch a chair from indoors if you like.'

'No, no, you're alright,' said Munro, concerned by her appearance. 'No offence, but you're looking awful tired Mrs Buchanan, are you okay?'

'I've not been sleeping, Inspector. How can I? Not knowing where he is?'

'You have my sympathies, it cannae be easy. Have you been out here all day?'

'Near enough.'

'And have you had yourself some supper or anything to drink?'

'No,' said Heather, staring blankly up the street, 'I'm not sure I can manage anything.'

'Look, come away inside and I'll put the kettle on, fetch you a bite to eat perhaps?'

'No, I can't go in. What if he comes by and I'm not here?'

'Mrs Buchanan,' said Munro softly, 'if you go on a hunger strike and catch a cold, you'll not be much good to anyone now, will you? We can leave the door open and sit by the window. How about it?'

Heather turned to face him and smiled limply.

'Aye, okay,' she said, 'ten minutes'll not do any harm I suppose.'

* * *

Munro busied himself in the kitchen as Heather settled into the armchair by the window, turning it slightly to ensure she had a good view down the street.

'You're very kind,' she said as Munro returned with two mugs of tea, 'I suppose you'll be wanting to ask some questions now you're here?'

'Aye, if that's okay with you. And after that I'll make you up a wee sandwich. Or perhaps you'd prefer some soup?'

'Let's see how we go, eh? So, what is it you'd like to know, Inspector?'

Munro set his mug on the table and unzipped his coat.

'Well, Mrs…'

'Och, Heather please. The name's Heather.'

'Heather. Okay. See here, Heather, I'm trying to paint a wee picture of the situation, you know, possible reasons behind your husband's sudden disappearance so you'll forgive me if the questions sound a little abrupt but for starters, do you and Angus have any money problems? I mean, financially speaking, are you okay?'

'Oh, we're more than okay,' said Heather, 'we're not millionaires mind, but we're comfortable. We dinnae have to think twice about paying a bill, if that's what you mean.'

'Aye, that's it. Good. And Angus. Health-wise, is he okay?'

'Yes, yes. He's no problems in that department. Did that young policeman not tell you that?'

'I didnae get the details I'm afraid, so…'

'The only thing my Angus can't do, Inspector, is stand still.'

'I'm glad to hear it,' said Munro, smiling as he sipped his tea. 'Tell me, I understand Angus owns a company called "Remus Trading". Is that right?'

'Remus? Oh aye, that was Angus alright.'

'And what does it trade in exactly?'

'Nothing. Not any more.'

'Sorry?' said Munro hiding his surprise, 'What do you mean; *not any more?*'

'They packed it in.'

'They?'

'Aye,' said Heather, 'Angus and Remo, it was the pair of them that ran it.'

'And that would be Remo Carducci?'

'It would.'

'Good friends, are they?'

'Oh aye, they're like brothers, known each other since forever.'

'Okay. So, Heather, this company, what was it used for? Buying and selling?'

'No, not really, more importing. Food mainly. From Italy.'

'Forgive me,' said Munro, 'but I'm a wee bit lost now. Food? From Italy?'

'Aye. You see Inspector, Angus and Remo used to work on the docks, right? Like everybody else they thought it was a job for life, then like everybody else they got laid off but Remo, well he was the lucky one, he had the family business to fall back on.'

'You mean the cafes?'

'No, no,' said Heather impatiently, 'that came later. See, when Remo's great grandfather settled here as a young man, he opened a fish and chip shop, then another, and another.'

'Go on.'

'Well, Remo had no interest in selling fish suppers for the rest of his life, no interest at all and as for Angus, well, he had to find a way of making some money so's he could keep a roof over his head. That's when he had his... what's the word I'm looking for? *Epiphany*. Clever man, my Angus.'

'What did he do?'

'He used his brains,' said Heather. 'See, there's only three things Remo's ever been interested in, Inspector:

women, wine and food. *Proper food*, he calls it, like spaghetti and meatballs. It's not to my liking but each to his own. Anyways, Angus told him straight, if he didnae want to be standing over a deep fat fryer for the next fifty years the only way forward was to expand his business; open a café or two and start dishing up the kind of food he wouldnae shut up about. The rest, as they say, is history. The very next day, with not a penny between them, they were off about the town looking for a site for the first cafe.'

'So Carducci's was all Angus's idea?' said Munro.

'Apart from the chip shops, aye.'

'So how does the import business fit it?'

'It's laughable really,' said Heather, smiling at the memory. 'They borrowed money left, right and centre to fit out the first café, that's the one on esplanade in Ayr, but they didnae think about stocking it. Remo needed proper Italian ingredients for the cooking and Angus had an idea to sell them in the café too, you know, like a wee delicatessen. Only trouble was you couldnae get your hands on things like that back then, not without paying through the nose for it. I mean folk round here had never even heard of *pesto,* let alone eaten it. So anyway, Remo went to Italy and came back with as much as he could. Took him a couple of weeks but it was worth the effort. I'd never have guessed Italian food could be so popular.'

'Quite the success then?' said Munro.

'Oh yes, Inspector, quite the success indeed,' said Heather. 'After that they paid a fellow with a van to go fetch the stuff for them. They'd send him off with a huge shopping list and strict instructions to get himself back as quick as possible: olive oil, tomatoes, anchovies, salami, cheese, everything. That's why they formed Remus. To make it official.'

'Now that is a fascinating story,' said Munro. 'Your husband's quite the entrepreneur. Aye, that's the word, *entrepreneur.* But tell me, if things were going so well, why on earth did they close the company?'

'Times changed Inspector,' said Heather with a remorseful sigh, 'the world's a much smaller place these days. You can get all that stuff in your local supermarket now.'

'Aye, you're not wrong there.'

'But hats off to them, it was good while it lasted. Do you know they even supplied Jenners in Edinburgh for a few years?'

'Is that so? It seems to me Mr Carducci has an awful lot to thank your husband for.'

'Oh aye, if it wasnae for Angus I've no doubt Remo and Anita would still be living above the chip shop but Remo knows that. Everything's split fifty-fifty. There's not a bad bone between them.'

Munro stood, picked up the empty mugs and headed for the kitchen.

'They must have a lot in common,' he said, 'to get on so well.'

'Right enough, golf and women. Especially the women,' said Heather raising her eyebrows, *window shopping* Angus calls it.'

'Och, I'm sure that's all it is. You know, I used to play the odd round of golf myself.'

'Is that so?' said Heather.

'Oh aye, gave it up though. Hitting a wee ball with a long stick wasnae something I excelled at.'

'Oh, you'd get on well with those two then, they're both rubbish but they must get some form of twisted pleasure from it.'

'Play locally do they?'

'No, no,' said Heather. 'Well, they used to. Until Remo started looking farther afield. It started with Kinsale then before you knew it they were off to Lisbon, then the Costa bloody del Sol. They've even been to Oslo. God knows where they'll end up next.'

'Well with time on their hands I suppose…'

'Too much time, Inspector. Every couple of months they're away. Still, can't complain, better than having him under my feet.'

'Right enough,' said Munro. 'Now, will I fetch you that sandwich? I'll not be happy unless I see you eat something.'

'You're alright, Inspector. I'll wait for Anita, that's Remo's wife, she'll be along soon.'

'So you'll not be alone?'

'No, no. She'll be stopping here all night.'

'Good,' said Munro, zipping his coat, 'perhaps some company will help take your mind off things. Well, that's me away then. I've kept you long enough.'

'It's been a pleasure.'

'And try not to fret too much, Heather. I know it's a big ask but rest assured, we'll find your husband. You have my word on that.'

* * *

The headlights cut a swathe through the dusky night sky as Munro, torn between returning to the office and heading home to Carsethorn, drove back along Dalhowan Street perturbed by the skeleton Angus Buchanan had hanging in his closet. He pulled over and called West, rankled by his own ambivalence.

'Charlie,' he said with a weary sigh, 'what's happening?'

'I'm dropping Dougal back at the office so he can get his scooter then we're off to mine. Where do you want to meet?'

'Carsethorn, I think. I'm not sure.'

'Carsethorn? Are you bonkers?' said West. 'By the time you get there the sun'll be coming up.'

'Aye, maybe,' said Munro, 'but I'm not in the mood for hotels, you know I cannae stand them.'

'What do you mean *hotels*? I've just moved in to a two bedroom flat, you can stay at mine.'

'No, no, I'll not impose. It's not…'

'Oi, Jimbo, you listen to me,' said West sternly, 'you've been good enough to let me crash at yours for weeks on end, rent free and you've haven't whinged about it. Not once. So the least you can do is let me return the favour, okay?'

Munro sat back and smiled.

'Aye, okay then,' he said. 'Just the one night, mind.'

'Good. I've got a fridge full of food and plenty of booze so put your foot down. We'll see you there.'

* * *

Dougal sat sipping a glass of orange juice like an eight-year-old on his best behaviour, nervous of making marks on the table or speaking out of turn. He watched as West wrestled with a bottle of Côtes du Rhone and was about to offer his help when the cork popped out with satisfying plop.

'This had better be worth the effort,' she said taking a gulp and gasping with relief.

'So he's definitely coming then, Miss?' said Dougal. 'The Boss?'

'Yup, he's on his way over now, shouldn't be long.'

'Pity he's not staying longer, we could use the help.'

'Oi, cheeky, what're you saying? That I'm not up to the job?'

'No, no,' said Dougal, 'I didnae mean…'

'I know what you meant, relax, I'm kidding you.'

'Sorry. So, do you think he'll hang around, you know, until the case is over?'

'He will if I have anything to do with it,' said West with a wink.

'Great. I like him. I mean he's funny but there's something solid about him, know what I mean? Something a wee bit *old fashioned*.'

'Probably his age.'

'You get on well, you two,' said Dougal inquisitively. 'How did you meet, if you dinnae mind me asking? Did you work together?'

'Yup. Going back a while now but I was with City of London, some bloke had disappeared, turned out he lived on James's patch in East London so I transferred there, temporarily. He led the investigation, thank God, or I probably wouldn't be here now.'

'What do you mean?'

West topped up her glass and sat down.

'Between you and me, I was in a hole, totally messed up,' she said. 'I hated my job, hated where I lived and I hated my fiancée. I found out he was bedding everything in sight except me so I broke it off and married a bottle of Smirnoff instead.'

'Sorry, Miss, I didnae mean to pry, I was just curious about…'

'Ancient history, Dougal, don't worry about it. If it wasn't for Jimbo, *DI Munro*, I'd probably be on the street or in a hostel. He sorted me out.'

'So he was like, well, a kind of mentor or a father figure then?'

'Yeah, I suppose so,' said West, smiling fondly, 'but come to think of it, no. Actually, he was more like a bloody sergeant major, put the boot in good and proper, metaphorically speaking that is. Anyway, enough about me, how was your weekend?'

'Och, no different to the rest of the week.'

'Really?' said West, as the entryphone buzzed. 'Thought you'd have been out clubbing or down the pub.'

'No, no, that's not for me. I like a good book or a crossword, anything that gets me thinking.'

'No love interest then? No future Mrs McCrae tucked away somewhere?'

'You are joking me?' said Dougal cynically. 'Unfortunately Miss, there's not too many lassies round here into fishing and sudoku.'

* * *

Munro, looking exhausted, loosened his tie as he ambled into the kitchen, slapped Dougal on the shoulder and slumped into a dining chair beside him.

'Alright, laddie,' he said with a smirk, 'has she got you on the vodka and orange already?'

'No, Boss, just juice. I'm driving. Well, scootering.'

'Good for you. Fortunately, I am not.'

'You look knackered,' said West, waving a wine glass in one hand and a bottle of Scotch in the other. 'What would you like?'

'I'll take a Balvenie for starters. Three fingers. Thanking you.'

Dougal raised his glass.

'Well, here's to you Miss,' he said. 'Good luck in your new home.'

'Oh thanks, Dougal, very kind of you.'

'Aye, I'll second that,' said Munro. 'Are you not stopping for supper, Dougal?'

'No, Boss, much as I'd like to I'm still full of the pizza and after this weekend, all I'm looking forward to right now is crawling into my pit.'

'Cannae blame you for that but before you go, how did you get on with Carducci?'

'Well,' said Dougal, knocking back his juice, 'I think we can forget about Romulus, he's not from Rome. His family home's a place called Avella, north of Naples.'

'Naples?' said Munro, 'Och well that's a reputation of its own, mainly involving men who like to make offers and the occasional horse's head of course.'

'And as for the bank account,' said West, 'as far as he knows it was closed when they rolled the company.'

'That's right,' said Dougal, pulling out his notebook 'and for the record Remus Trading had two directors: Carducci and Buchanan. Angus Buchanan was also secretary and it was registered to his home address in Crosshill. The company was dissolved nineteen months ago.'

'Nineteen months? That's relatively recent,' said Munro draining his glass, 'but if nothing else it corroborates Heather's version of events. I'm worried about her, she's not herself. She's taken this awful hard.'

'So has Carducci,' said West, as she slid a glass of red towards him, 'but that's not surprising either considering the amount of time they've known each other.'

Munro took a large sip of wine, leaned back and closed his eyes, a delicate frown creasing his forehead as he gathered his thoughts.

'Okay,' he said. 'According to Miss McClure at the bank, money's been paid into that account on a pretty regular basis for a while now so we need to find out where those deposits came from, sums that large have to leave a paper trail, right? Second, if the account's active then the bank must be sending statements somewhere so…'

'Yeah but hold on,' said West, 'surely they'd go to the registered address? In Crosshill? So either Carducci, his wife or Heather must know about it.'

'Aye, you'd think so,' said Munro, 'but not necessarily, a registered office and a trading address are two different things. Let's have a word with Miss McClure and find out where they're going. Dougal, something else. I'm not familiar with the current price of a new sports cars but I've a feeling you'd have to sell an awful lot of lasagne to drive a fancy vehicle like Carducci. Find out what you can about him. Got that?'

'Got it,' said Dougal as he pulled on his jacket and grabbed his helmet from the worktop, 'does this, er, does this mean you'll be in the office tomorrow, Boss?'

'Good grief, Dougal, does the phrase *standing on your own two feet* not mean anything to you? We'll see, laddie. We'll see.'

Chapter 6

Due largely to the pressures of work and a love-life that resembled a scrambled egg, West, once proud of her ability to rustle up a first-class meal at the drop of a hat, had long since placed any aspirations about returning to the kitchen on the back burner, succumbing instead to the dubious delight of dining out on double cheeseburgers, chicken chow mein and shish kebabs seven nights a week. She regarded the cooker with a look of trepidation normally reserved for people she knew but failed to recognise as she struggled to reacquaint herself with the hob.

Munro, his senses heightened by the smell of burning bacon, smiled broadly as he glided swiftly through the lounge and flung open the doors to the balcony.

'I'll take mine crispy,' he said, 'but I think you'll find it's already smoked.'

'If you can do better, you're welcome to try,' said a frustrated West as the eggs spluttered in the frying pan, 'otherwise make yourself useful and lay the table.'

Munro obligingly obeyed and sat with his arms folded as she tossed a handful of charcoaled rashers onto his plate.

'Might not look great,' she said, grabbing a couple of slices from the toaster, 'but it'll taste fine, I'm sure. What's up? Something wrong with the toast?'

'No, no, it matches the bacon perfectly.'

West glowered across the table before laughing aloud.

'Sorry, pretty crap isn't it?'

'Nothing of the sort,' said Munro as he tucked into a runny yolk, 'I've had worse, mainly by own hand.'

West glanced at him furtively as she slapped a bottle of ketchup.

'So, er, what time are you heading back?' she said.

Munro stopped chewing, a look of mild surprise on his face.

'Well,' he said, clearing his throat. 'I hadnae… I'll finish my breakfast first, if that's okay with you?'

'Yeah whatever, there's no rush. I'm not even meant to be working today but I thought I should nip over later and check on Dougal. What do you think?'

'Aye, sounds like a plan but you dinnae have to clear it with me, lassie.'

'I know but I was thinking… you could come too, if you fancy it.'

'No, no. I should get going, the garden needs watering and then there's…'

'Hold on,' said West as she reached for her phone, 'sorry. It's Dougal. He's up early.'

'Best see what he wants, lassie, might be important.'

Munro cleared away the plates and set about making a brew as West took the call.

'Dougal, what's up?' she said, crunching through a slice of toast.

'Morning, Miss, sorry to bother you so early but I need a wee favour.'

'If I can, I will. Go on.'

'Well, thing is see,' said Dougal, sounding flustered, 'I've already been onto the bank to request details on that

Remus account and now I'm doing some digging on Mr Carducci but the Chief's just come in and…'

'And?'

'There's been a car abandoned and we've no-one free to take a look at it and I cannae keep jumping from one job to another or I'll not get anything done so I was wondering, would you mind…?'

'No sweat,' said West, 'is it far?'

'Just off the B744 from Belston towards the Auchincruive Estate, fifteen minutes tops. Uniform are in attendance. I'll pop along later if I can.'

* * *

'I take it he's not suffering from insomnia,' said Munro, handing West a mug of tea.

'No. Car's been abandoned on the Auchin-something estate.'

'What? Well, that's not for the likes of you, let uniform deal with it.'

'They are apparently but DCI Elliot's asked Dougal to take a gander. That's why he rang, he's up to his eyeballs and wondered if we'd take a look instead.'

'We?'

'Well, alright. Me.'

'Hold on,' said Munro, 'you say DCI Elliot asked Dougal to take a look?'

'Yup. Why? Does that mean something?'

'Aye, it means it's not just an abandoned car, Charlie. There's more to it than that. Trust me.'

'So what is it then, this estate? Like council houses or something?'

Munro swigged his tea and shook his head despondently.

'No. Well not yet, anyway,' he said. 'It's an old country estate, six hundred acres of prime woodland teeming with wildlife but it'll not be long before they rip it up, cover it with tarmac and stick a load of houses in its place.'

'That's criminal.'

'That's progress.'

'Well in that case,' said West, 'it'd be nice to see it before the developers move in. What do you reckon, you up for it? Be a chance to get out, bit of fresh air?'

Munro finished his tea and sighed submissively.

'Aye okay, go on then. On one condition.'

'Name it.'

'We take my car. I'll not fit in that go-kart of yours.'

West smiled, grabbed her coat and paused as her phone rang again.

'Dougal no doubt,' she said, 'probably forgotten…'

Munro looked on as she stared at the screen, the colour draining from her cheeks.

'What's wrong, Charlie?' he said, concerned by the troubled look on her face. 'It's not Dougal, is it? Are you okay?'

'Yeah, fine.'

* * *

Unlike his colleagues – most of whom looked forward to apprehending gangs of armed robbers, arresting suspected drug dealers or pursuing joyriders at high speed along the A77 – PC Ross Anderson preferred any task that kept him out of danger and away from his desk.

Leaning against the patrol car with his hands in his pockets and his cap perched jauntily on the back of his head he smirked at the sight of Munro's ageing Peugeot trundling sedately down the lane and, concluding it posed no imminent threat, turned away and lit another cigarette as it slowly ground to a halt behind the abandoned vehicle.

'I'm not one to gloat,' said Munro, nodding in the direction of the ambulance parked on the opposite side of the road, 'but that's not here as a precaution.'

West released her seat belt and opened the door.

'Come on then,' she said, 'what are we waiting for?'

'We're surveying the scene,' said Munro as he folded his arms and placed one hand on his chin, 'so tell me

Charlie, what do you see? Let's start with the car in question.'

West pulled the door shut and stared dead ahead, frowning as she concentrated on a description.

'Toyota Prius,' she said. 'Silver. Three years old and judging by the sign obscuring the rear window, it's obviously a taxi cab – Kestrel Cars.'

'Good. What else?'

'Well,' said West, hesitating, 'apart from the fact that the windows are misted up, it's a saloon, it's got five doors, four wheels…'

'Forget the car, look at the situation.'

'Sorry, Jimbo, you'll have to enlighten me.'

'See here, Charlie, there's no tyre marks on the road which means it wasnae travelling at speed and it didnae brake hard. The hedge hasnae been damaged either so the chances of it being run off the road are probably zero. Now, look at the grass beneath the wheels, it's only been flattened where the car's mounted the verge, there's been no shilly-shallying in an attempt to park it safely. No, no, that motor car was placed there in a deliberate and precise manner.'

'I could've told you that,' said West, 'eventually.'

Munro lowered the window as PC Anderson stubbed out his cigarette with the toe of his boot, straightened his cap and ambled towards them.

'Morning, Sir,' he said, 'you can't stop here I'm afraid, as you can see we're conducting an investigation.'

'Glad to hear it, laddie,' said Munro as he flashed his warrant card and stepped from the car, 'so, what've you got? Apart from time on your hands, that is.'

Anderson smiled and gave a nonchalant shrug of the shoulders.

'Well, the vehicle was dumped here some time in the early hours, I'd say. A fella on his way to the veterinary college reported it this morning.'

'Time?'

'Let me see,' said Anderson as he pulled a tattered notebook from his breast pocket, '5.42am. I got here just after six.'

'Okay. And do we know who the owner is?'

'Oh aye. I called Kestrel Cars, they've an office on Smith Street in the town centre. They own the vehicle but the driver on duty was a Mr Tomek Dubrowski, I think that's Polish. The fella at the cab company says he's been trying to reach him since last Thursday cos he wants his car back but he's not answering his phone.'

'And he didn't think to call the police about it?' said West.

'I think he thought the better of it, Miss. Seems Mr Dubrowski's terms of employment weren't exactly legit.'

'I see,' said Munro, 'I'd have a wee word with him about that if I were you. Does he have an address?'

'He rents a room on Souter Place, Sir. The lads are round there now, see if they can't raise him from his pit.'

'Anything else we should know about?' said West, pulling on a pair of gloves.

'The car's not locked and the keys are in the ignition.'

'And I take it nothing's been touched?' said Munro.

'No, Sir. Well I mean, I had to open the door to take a wee peek inside but that's it.'

'Most efficient, Constable…?'

'Anderson, Sir.'

'Tell me, Anderson,' said Munro as he walked towards the car, 'would you happen to know why DCI Elliot is so interested in this and not your Super?'

'I reckon it's probably something to do with what's in the back, Sir.'

Munro, one hand on the door handle, regarded Anderson with a curious tilt of the head as he gently eased it open. Having instinctively established that the presence of an ambulance was no coincidence, the sight of the body slumped across the back seat came as no surprise. West squeezed by the hedge and opened the door on the opposite side, her lip curling as she came to face to face with the wide-eyed cadaver.

'Blimey,' she said, 'he doesn't look too happy.'

'Not surprising,' said Munro, 'probably wasn't planning on being dropped off at the Pearly Gates.'

'So what do you think? Heart attack?'

'Possibly, but going by the expression on his face I'd say he's either bitten into a lemon or he's suffered a stroke. My money's on the latter.'

'Really? I didn't know a stroke could kill you?'

'It could if it's a side effect of something else. There's some bruising to his cheeks too. Mild.'

'So he wasn't punched.'

'No, no, it's not that severe. It looks as though somebody covered his mouth with their hands, as if they were trying to shut him up. Your turn.'

'Okay,' said West, 'off the top of my head a couple of scenarios spring to mind.'

'Go on.'

'Well apart from the bruising there's no sign of a struggle, no footprints or scuff marks on the seats so I reckon he either pegged it here, quite suddenly, or he was already dead and brought here later. Either way the driver wasn't bothered about calling an ambulance and probably legged it, either intentionally or through fear.'

'Good,' said Munro, 'but if this gentleman had already expired, do you not think tossing him in the river with a few bricks for company would've been a better way to dispose of him?'

'So you're saying if he was killed beforehand, if it wasn't a cardiac, then the killer wanted us to find him?'

'Aye, lassie. It's certainly a possibility. Why else would he leave it here? Okay, let's move on, what else?'

'Clothes,' said West. 'He's casually dressed, a bit under-dressed in fact so I'd say he was a local fare, probably… where are you going?'

Munro, not familiar with the concept of travelling by taxi at two in the morning wearing nothing but shirt-sleeves went to the rear of the car, popped open the boot and smiled knowingly at the expensive-looking leather holdall.

'On you go,' he said, 'let's see what we've got.'

West gave him a sideways glance, slowly unzipped it and pulled the contents from the bag as if conducting an inventory.

'Blouson jacket, cream,' she said. 'Socks, five pairs. Underpants, five pairs. Shirts, five of. Why do I get the feeling he was going away for five days?'

'That'll be your sixth sense, Charlie.'

'Toiletry bag containing… one razor, one toothbrush, one tube of… oh, and a wallet,' said West, flipping it open, 'now who would keep their wallet in a toiletry bag?'

'Someone who was hiding it,' said Munro.

'Can't think why, it's empty. I mean no cash, just a couple of cards. Visa debit and a Mastercard. Name's Lars Gundersen and look, they've even got his photo on the back.'

'Well at least we know who he is.'

'DNB Bank. You heard of them?'

'No, I have not,' said Munro, 'but with a name like Gundersen he's no doubt Scandinavian. Bag, Charlie. Side pocket.'

West eagerly opened it up and retrieved a sheaf of travel documents.

'Spot on,' she said, opening a passport. 'He's Norwegian. Age: sixty-four. Doesn't show an address though.'

'Look for the personal identification number, you'll have to contact the authorities and give them that, then you'll get all the details you need.'

'Okay.'

'What else?'

'According to this,' said West, 'he was booked on a cruise aboard the Boudicca, a tour of the fjords. Inside cabin, single berth, leaving Greenock… yesterday.'

'Well he's certainly missed that boat.'

'Hold on, it says here the cruise is eight days.'

'So?'

'He's only got five of everything.'

'Then there's a reason,' said Munro, rubbing the back of his neck. 'Has he an itinerary amongst that lot?'

'Yup.'

'Day five. Would they be at sea or does the boat dock somewhere?'

'Day five… oh clever man. Bergen. It docks in Bergen, late morning.'

'Then I'd wager Charlie, that that's where Mr Gundersen planned to jump ship.'

'Jump ship? Why would he…?'

'Sshh,' said Munro raising his hand, 'listen… if I'm not mistaken, *that* is the sound of a giant Asian hornet.'

West looked up and smiled as Dougal, squinting against the breeze in his open-face helmet, came whizzing down the road on his Vespa and parked beside them.

'Got here as quick as I could,' he said, wiping a tear from the corner of his eye, 'have I missed much?'

'Nah, not really,' said West, 'just a dead Norwegian in the back of a taxi. Seen one, you've seen them all.'

'Bit far from home, is he not?' said Dougal, grinning as he removed his helmet, 'not exactly the tourist trail round here.'

'Quite right,' said Munro, 'so you have to ask yourself the question: what was he doing here? Particularly as he'd booked himself a wee cruise which left yesterday.'

'Search me, visiting friends maybe?'

'Maybe. Okay you two, listen up, a few words before I go…'

'Go?' said West. 'Go where?'

'Home of course. You forget I'm not a part of your team.'

'Bugger.'

'You need to get SOCOs up here as soon as possible, they need to go over the car and then the lane, from top to bottom. Second, the college is up the way there, go see if they captured anything on their cameras, anyone behaving like a badger in the dead of night. Got that?'

'Aye,' said Dougal despondently, 'not much then.'

'Och, I'm not finished yet, laddie,' said Munro, 'all the stuff in the boot, forensics. Kestrel cars; find out when our friend booked his ride and where they picked him up from. Oh, and you need to get Mr Gundersen here off for an exploratory at the mortuary before he goes completely stiff.'

'Is that it?' said West, sarcastically.

'Norwegian authorities,' said Munro with a wink and a nod, 'you need an address for our visitor, see if you can trace a next of kin and just for good measure, you may as well check on the state of his finances. I cannae see anyone going on their holidays without some cash in their wallet. Should keep you busy for a day or two.'

'You're not wrong there,' said Dougal, sighing as he wandered towards the taxi, 'I'm just gonna take a wee look, okay?'

West folded her arms and glanced sheepishly at Munro.

'You've got to give me a lift back so I can get my car, right?' she said, shuffling aimlessly and kicking the dirt beneath her feet. 'So I was thinking, how about we stop at the shopping centre on the way, pick you up a couple of shirts and then you could…'

'No, no, no, lassie,' said Munro, laughing as he reached for his car keys, 'you're not getting me involved with this one Charlie, I've told you several times, you're more than capable of…'

'Boss!'

Munro looked up as Dougal frantically beckoned them to the taxi.

'What is it laddie? Can you not see I'm trying my best to wheedle out of this investigation?'

'This fella, Boss, he's not a Norwegian. He's Angus Buchanan.'

Chapter 7

West, looking as smug as the cat that got the cream, held up two cellophane-wrapped shirts, one dark blue, the other plain white as Munro – reminded of the interminably tedious shopping trips he used to make with his dearly departed wife – sighed in defeat.

'I'll take the white,' he said, 'short sleeves.'

'We'd better get two,' said West with a smile, 'and how about a nice jumper, in case it gets chilly?'

'No thank you. I've been thinking about that taxi…'

'A cardigan then?'

'No thank you. It's a Prius…'

'Underwear's over there. Long socks or short?'

'Short. And a Prius is a…'

'Do you need a hat?'

'Charlie!' said Munro under his breath. 'If I had to compile a list of things I hate most in life, shopping for clothes would be at number two, right between garlic and chilli sauce, and number four would be those folk who dinnae pay attention when somebody's talking to them.'

'Sorry, just trying to help.'

Munro grabbed a three-pack of socks and shorts, relieved West of the shirts and headed for the till.

'As I was saying…' he said, tucking the receipt into his wallet.

'You could claim for those,' said West, 'on expenses. Sorry.'

'…the taxi's a Toyota Prius. It's a hybrid.'

'Meaning?'

'Meaning if it was driven in electric mode it could easily have slinked by Carducci's place and nobody would have heard a thing.'

'Of course! So it was waiting for Buchanan all along and when he popped out to get the wine, they snatched him.'

'No, no,' said Munro. 'Angus Buchanan wasnae abducted Charlie. I'm telling you, that taxi was booked to pick him up at a particular time. The bottle of wine was just a ruse to get him out of the house.'

'Okay. But what about the bag in the boot?' said West. 'If he had plans to abscond how did he get the bag in the boot? He'd have had to have taken it with him to Carducci's gaff so surely his wife would've known about it?'

Munro paused as they left the department store.

'It's only a theory,' he said, 'but let's just imagine for a moment it was already there.'

'In the boot? But how?'

'Perhaps he knew the driver. Perhaps he'd given him the bag the day before.'

'Or,' said West, her face lighting up as she wagged her finger, 'maybe that bag wasn't his at all. Maybe it was packed *for* him, specifically for the trip.'

'At last, Charlie,' said Munro, smiling as he pulled his wailing phone from his pocket, 'you're beginning to think like a detective. I dinnae recognise this number.'

'Just answer it, you never know, it might be a good deal on double-glazing.'

'Munro. Who is this please?'

'Inspector,' came a sultry but confident voice. 'Miss McClure. The Clydesdale Bank. I've been trying to contact you, are you not in the habit of answering your phone?'

'Not really, it's always bad news. How can I help you Miss McClure?'

'I've some rather important information about that account we were discussing, Remus Trading? Perhaps you'd care to drop by?'

'Aye, okay,' said Munro. 'Give me twenty minutes.'

'Not double-glazing then?' said West as he terminated the call.

'No Charlie, it was that Miss McClure at the…'

'Ooh, get in there, Jimbo. Somebody's after your…'

'Good grief, Charlie, I never realised you were so in touch with your inner child. Come on, I'll drop you at the office. If they've picked up the taxi driver then I suggest you start questioning him. I'll be back as soon as I can.'

* * *

Munro – expecting to find Miss McClure seated behind her desk wearing the same vintage outfit and dour expression he'd familiarised himself with the day before – was taken aback at the sight of her poised by the window clad in a snug-fitting, knee-length pencil skirt and a crisp, burgundy blouse unbuttoned at the neck, looking, to all intents and purposes, like somebody off on a rather expensive lunch date.

'Something wrong, Inspector?' she said, smiling warmly.

'No, no,' said Munro, clearing his throat, 'you look… busy. I hope I've not kept you waiting, I had to deal with a Norwegian in a taxi.'

'Sounds intriguing,' said McClure.

'Aye, are you familiar with the name Edvard Munch?'

'Why of course. You're not telling me you found Edvard Munch in a taxi, surely?'

'No, no, it was "The Scream".'

'I'm sorry?'

'Ignore me. So, Miss McClure, you said you had some information for me?'

'That's right, Inspector. Coffee? It's only filter from the pot but it's quite palatable.'

'Aye, very kind,' said Munro, 'white, three sugars. Thanking you.'

McClure handed him a cup and returned to her desk.

'As I mentioned earlier, I sent you an email, or rather, I sent it to your colleague.'

'I'm sure I'll get around to reading it next time I'm suffering from a bout of terminal boredom. What of it?'

'Here,' said McClure, handing him a sheet of paper. 'I've printed it off for you. As you can see quite a substantial sum was transferred from the Remus account late last night and again early this morning.'

'Two payments of twenty-five grand?' said Munro, aghast. 'By jiminy, that's more than I earn in a… what's with the times? Why just before midnight and just after?'

'There's a daily limit on the amount that can be transferred, Inspector…'

'Of course there is,' said Munro. 'I see there's no mention in your email of where the money was transferred to? Is there a reason for that?'

'Security, Inspector,' said McClure, 'but now that you're here I can tell you that the money was transferred to an account held with DNB. That's a bank in Norway.'

'DNB?' said Munro. 'This account, wouldnae be a Mr Lars Gundersen by any chance, would it?'

'Indeed it would, Inspector. How clever of you. I can see I'll have to get up early if I'm to catch you out.'

'Earlier than you think,' said Munro, muttering under his breath. 'Listen, Miss McClure, I cannae thank you enough for this, you've been most helpful and I appreciate it but I need one more favour from you.'

McClure, elbows on table, clasped her hands beneath her chin and regarded Munro with a seductive smile.

'I wonder what that could be, Inspector?' she said softly.

'Remus Trading. I need to know what address you have for them, I mean, where the statements and any correspondence is being sent.'

'Oh I've told you before, Inspector, I'm not at liberty to divulge such…'

'Miss McClure,' said Munro impatiently as he fixed her with an icy stare, 'no offence, but I've a murder on my hands and whoever runs the Remus account might be mixed up in it, and I simply dinnae have the time to jump through hoops just so I can…'

'Okay,' said McClure holding up her hands, 'but if anyone asks…'

'I'll not forget this, I owe you.'

'Quid pro quo, Inspector?' said McClure as she tapped away on the keyboard.

'Aye, if you like. What is it? Have you a wee parking ticket that needs sorting?'

McClure sat back and stared at Munro with a mischievous twinkle in her eye.

'There's no parking ticket but you do strike me as the kind of man who'd enjoy a decent Bordeaux and some Schubert, Inspector.'

'Well, the Bordeaux perhaps, but the Schubert's open to debate.'

'Good. I was wondering, I don't suppose you'd care to join me for a glass or two, perhaps? I've some vintage…'

'I'm afraid I shall have to decline, Miss McClure. Nothing personal but I'm knee deep in an investigation at the moment and…'

'You're not married are you?'

'Widowed.'

'Well surely just a…'

'And I'm more of a Leonard Cohen man myself.'

'Why so am I!' said McClure, 'I've a few of his records, on vinyl no less. We could listen to those instead.'

Munro stood, zipped his jacket and smiled.

'I admire your persistence, Miss McClure,' he said, grinning. 'but if you've any ideas about tying me to a kitchen chair in an attempt to draw a hallelujah from my lips, I'm afraid it's not going to happen. Not tonight anyway.'

'Pity,' said McClure with a sly grin. 'The address you want. It's Dalhowan Street.'

* * *

Tomek Dubrowski – with his shaved head, stocky build and a face like a potato that came second in a fight with a mallet – looked as though he'd spent most of his adult life toiling in a Gulag under a sentence of hard labour. Unfazed by the stark surroundings of the interview room he sat with his arms folded and smiled in an annoyingly relaxed manner at the two police officers glaring back at him from across the desk.

'Do you understand why you're here?' said PC Anderson.

'Yes,' said Dubrowski, nodding a little too enthusiastically, 'I think so.'

'*Think so* isn't good enough,' said West. 'Would you like an interpreter?'

'No. I can speak English.'

'In that case, Mr Dubrowski, you're being held on suspicion of theft, abandoning a vehicle, abduction, and concealing or failing to report a death, so once again, do you understand?'

'Yes.'

'Okay,' said West, 'let's start at the beginning. How long have you been here? In the United Kingdom?'

'For two years.'

'And you have a bedsit in Souter Place?'

'Yes, this is correct. And some nights I stay with my girlfriend.'

'Girlfriend?' said Anderson.

'Yes, she is very nice, has important job. I think she likes me.'

'Or maybe she just feels sorry for you,' said West brusquely.

'This is possible too.'

'So where are you from Mr Dubrowski?'

'Polska. Poland.'

'And do you have a passport?'

'Nie.'

'I mean a Polish passport?'

'Nie. But I have identity papers. The other policemen are taking it.'

'How about a National Insurance number?' said Anderson.

'Nie.'

'So you've not been claiming any welfare benefits since you arrived in this country?'

'Nie.'

West, irked by Dubrowski's insolent smile, leaned back in her chair, making no attempt to conceal her distaste for his seemingly arrogant attitude.

'What do you do for money, Mr Dubrowski?' she said accusingly. 'How do you buy food or pay bills or your rent?'

'I do many works,' he said, 'all different. The peoples I am working for pay me cash.'

'I see,' said Anderson, smirking as he sensed a guilty charge, 'and are you aware that that is illegal?'

'Yes. I am caught. It's okay.'

Anderson glanced at West and scratched the back of his head, flabbergasted at Dubrowski's almost surreal sense of honesty.

'Kestrel Cars,' said West, tapping her biro on the desk. 'How long have you been working for Kestrel Cars?'

'It's not long,' said Dubrowski. 'One month maybe.'

'And they pay you cash as well?'

'Yes.'

'Dear, dear, dear,' said Anderson, 'seems like they're in a whole heap of trouble too. Do you make a habit of biting the hand that feeds you, Mr Dubrowski?'

'Biting hand?'

'You drive for Kestrel, they pay you, that's how it works. So why steal their vehicle? Have you been taking fares without telling them?'

'No. Of course not. Well, one or two maybe.'

'Great, that's another one to add to the list. So, when were you planning to return the vehicle?'

'I was going to take it back tomorrow. I don't have car. I thought one or two days, they won't mind so much.'

West slammed her pen on the desk, stood with a sigh and began pacing the room, forcing Dubrowski to swivel in his seat in an attempt to follow her.

'Well, that's where you're wrong,' she said, stopping directly behind him, 'they mind very much indeed. How do you know Lars Gundersen?'

'What is Lars?' said Dubrowski.

'What is Lars?' said West. 'Lars is the man we found in the back of your taxi. Lars is the *dead* man we found in the back of your taxi.'

'Ah, him. I did not know he was…'

'He was what?' said Anderson. 'Lars? There? Dead?'

'Where did you pick him up?' said West, cutting in.

'In street.'

'Really?'

'Yes really. Man telephones me, tells me to collect him at exactly three-thirty and take him to ship.'

'So it wasn't Kestrel that called you?'

'Nie.'

'And it wasn't Mr Gundersen?'

'Nie. It was other man. He says he will pay me when I arrive at boat.'

'What other man?' said West as she returned to her seat. 'Who will pay you?'

'The man who telephones me. He gives me lots of works.'

'His name?'

'I don't know,' said Dubrowski shrugging his shoulders, 'he is not telling me his name.'

'Where does he live?'

'I don't know. I am just doing the driving for him. He tells me where to go, what I must collect and where I must take it. Then I collect monies for the work.'

'Where?' said Anderson, intrigued by the turn of events. 'Where do you collect the money from?'

'Always is somewhere different. Sometimes waste paper bin on street, sometimes in toilet of pub…'

'And you don't think that's suspicious?'

'Yes of course, but is work and pays good monies.'

'How does he contact you?' said West.

'He telephones me.'

'At home or do you have a mobile?'

'I have mobile phone. Would you like to see? Here.'

Dubrowski took the phone from his back pocket, leaned forward and pushed it across the desk towards her.

'Which number is his?' she said scrolling through the history.

'Is top of the list, he is the last person who telephones me.'

'Good. We'll need to hold on to this, okay?' said West.

'Yes of course, is okay.'

'So, going back, you got a phone call from the mystery man and you were told to pick up Lars Gundersen. Where?'

'In village called Crosshill.'

'He was waiting for you?'

'Yes,' said Dubrowski, 'It was what you call the perfect timing. He comes from house just as I am arriving.'

'Did you speak?'

'Nie.'

'So tell me,' said West, 'Why didn't you take him to the docks? Why did you abort the journey and abandon the vehicle?'

Dubrowski bowed his head and sighed.

'I… he… he said he had pain, that he's not breathing correctly. I panic, I…'

'Oh come off it,' said West, 'I wasn't born yesterday Mr Dubrowski. You picked him around three-thirty, it wouldn't have taken you more than twenty minutes to reach Auchincruive, but you didn't go straight there, did you? There's a gap of almost twelve hours you haven't accounted for so, what did you do?'

Dubrowski raised his eyes to the ceiling, hesitating as he floundered for an answer.

'I panic,' he said. 'What to do with dead man? I go home and wait.'

'Unbelievable,' said West, 'so you didn't think to call an ambulance?'

'Nie. If I tell them I have dead man in taxi they ask me questions and call the police and then maybe they are sending me home. To Polska. This is right, yes?'

'Aye, quite possibly,' said Anderson. 'So, what about the bag in the boot?'

'Bag? I know nothing about a bag.'

'Is that so? Then perhaps you can tell us who gave you this?'

Anderson produced a clear plastic bag filled with bank notes and placed it on the table.

'For the record, Miss,' he said glancing at West, 'they found this on him during the search when they brought him in.'

'Where did you get this?' said West as she examined the sealed pouch.

Dubrowski, his eyes flitting between Anderson and West, wiped his nose with the back of his hand and hesitated before answering.

'That is what man pays me for works.'

'I'm losing my patience now,' said West. 'You never made it to the docks, you never put Gundersen on the boat, so you never got paid, did you? Last chance.'

'It is my monies, I am saving little now, for…'

'You're saving Norwegian kroner? How much is here?'

'Ten grand, Miss,' said Anderson, 'that's about a grand in sterling.'

'Incredible. Okay, I'll refresh your memory for you, shall I, Mr Dubrowski? You found the money in Gundersen's wallet which was in the bag in the boot of the car. Right?'

Dubrowski stopped smiling and lowered his head.

'Take him away, Constable,' said West, 'you can charge him with vehicle theft, robbery and failing to report a death. With any luck by this time tomorrow we'll be adding abduction and murder to the list.'

* * *

West, desperate for something to eat, trudged her way wearily up the stairs from the basement and groaned with despair as a middle-aged lady, obviously lost, accosted her by reception.

'Excuse me,' she said, 'sorry, dinnae mean to bother you but do you work here?'

West's shoulders slumped as she turned to face the smartly-dressed woman.

'Unfortunately, yes. How can I help, madam?'

'I was told my friend was here, would you happen to know where he is?'

'I'm afraid you'll have to give me more than that,' said West.

'Sorry, my head's mince. Tomek. His name's Tomek Dubrowski. His boss says he was brought here just this morning.'

West, her curiosity roused by the seemingly unlikely pairing, raised her eyebrows and regarded her inquiringly.

'And you are?'

'Clare. Clare MacAllister.'

'I'm Detective Sergeant West. Mind if I ask you a few questions, Clare?'

'Aye, ask away but do you mind if we sit down, these heels are killing me. So, is he here then? Is he in some kind of bother?'

'Tell you what,' said West, 'how about we stick to me asking the questions for now, it'll be quicker that way.'

'Sorry. On you go.'

'Thanks. So, how long have you known Tomek?'

'Och a wee while now. Just over a year I reckon.'

'And am I right in thinking he's your… partner or boyfriend?'

'Are you joking me?' said MacAllister laughing. 'Where'd you get that from? Listen, he's nice to be with but he's not marriage material, if you know what I'm saying.'

'I'm not sure I do.'

'Look, Sergeant, I'm getting on, I'm single. Tomek's just a wee bit of fun, okay?'

'Gotcha. And how long have the two of you been having fun together?'

'Oh, that's a recent thing,' said MacAllister, 'a few months maybe but I had a feeling it would happen sooner or later. He's this look about him, you know? Something a wee bit… dangerous.'

'You're not wrong there,' said West. 'How did you meet?'

'Work.'

'Work? Sorry, but if you don't me saying so, you don't strike me as the kind of person who'd move in the same circles as someone like Tomek.'

MacAllister squinted at West and tapped the side of her nose as if imparting some profound piece of wisdom.

'Every ship needs a captain, Sergeant,' she said, 'and every ship needs someone in the boiler room, too.'

'I see,' said West, 'and this ship would be?'

'Sorry, the restaurant of course. I'm the manager. Tomek used to work in the kitchen as a washer-upper.'

'Used to?'

'That's right, he's not with us anymore.'

'Why not?'

'Well I gave him a trial period to start with, casual like, you know, cash in hand and I was impressed. He worked awful hard, not a complaint about anything so I thought I'd take him on, permanently.'

'Well, he must've been made up about that, right?'

'Aye you'd think so,' said MacAllister, 'except Tomek didnae have the right, what shall we say, *documentation*, so he left. Pity but it's all his own fault. There's ways of doing things, Sergeant, the right way and the wrong way.'

'You don't say,' said West, sighing as she realised the conversation was going nowhere, 'so what did he do after that?'

'Oh, bits and bobs but he got himself a wee taxi job just recently. I think he's doing okay with that.'

'Good for him,' said West as she stood to leave, her mind wandering with thoughts of lunch, 'just out of interest, Miss MacAllister, this restaurant where you work, where Tomek worked, is it here?'

'No, no, but it's not far. Prestwick.'

'Oh right, not one of those overpriced places at the airport, is it? Twenty quid for a cheese roll?'

'No, no,' said MacAllister, laughing, 'it's not one of them. It's in town. Carducci's.'

Chapter 8

Lunch for Dougal was – more often than not – a predictably boring affair comprising beef or tuna paste sandwiches on thick, white bread which he'd prepared himself, wrapped in tin foil and sealed in a Tupperware box a few hours earlier. The spontaneity of having a toastie foisted upon him with no prior knowledge of the contents increased his appetite ten-fold. He dusted the crumbs from his fingers, tossed the papers in the bin and wiped the satisfied smile on his face with a paper napkin.

'Thanking you, Boss,' he said appreciatively, 'it's been a while since I had one of those. Went down a treat.'

'You're more than welcome, Dougal,' said Munro. 'Perhaps by way of recompense you'd care to make a brew.'

'Coming up.'

'Did you find anything on Carducci?'

'I certainly did,' said Dougal, 'I found having a name like Carducci makes my job a heck of a lot easier. That Porsche he drives, it's not his, it's a lease but like you said, he'd still have to sell a shedload of lasagne to pay for it.'

'Is that so?'

'Aye, costs over a grand a month.'

'A fool and his money,' said Munro. 'Anything else?'

'Not really, well, nothing out of the ordinary. They've been on their holidays. Three times this year already…'

'Three?' said Munro, surprised. 'And that's not out of the ordinary? Dear God, I'm lucky if I get two days in Auld Reekie. And that's in a caravan. Anywhere nice?'

'Cannae say, I've not been myself. Italy mainly.'

'Perhaps it's something to do with his family.'

'There's something else, Boss,' said Dougal as he filled the teapot. 'The passport Buchanan was carrying, you know, in the name of Lars Gundersen?'

'Go on.'

'I got the Royal Norwegian Embassy in London to run a check on it and they say it's legit. I've even got an address for him. It's an apartment in a place called Loddefjord, a suburb of Bergen.'

'Bergen?' said Munro, 'Well, that's where Buchanan or Gundersen appeared to be heading so it makes sense.'

'Aye, but here's the thing,' said Dougal, frowning as he scratched the back of his head, 'I did some research on Loddefjord and to be honest it's not the kind of place you'd buy a holiday home; high unemployment, lots of council housing and a problem with substance abuse that makes Glasgow look like a centre of abstinence.'

'Really?'

'Aye, so I've sent his details to the Hordaland District Police. Maybe they've heard of him. It's just that, I don't know, it's just not the kind of place someone like Mr Buchanan would be associated with.'

'Right enough,' said Munro, 'but perhaps his alter-ego has a darker side. Let me know if they find anything untoward. Now, I've just had a very interesting meeting with…'

Munro paused as West stumbled through the door, the stressed look on her face dissipating as she spied the brown paper carrier bag sitting on the desk.

'Jimbo, you're back!' she said as she moved towards it, 'is that…'

'Aye. All yours. Sausage and brown sauce.'

'God, I could kiss you, my stomach was beginning to think my throat had been cut. You not having any?'

'I've had two,' said Munro.

'Blimey, you've got a healthy appetite.'

'Not half as healthy as that Miss McClure.'

'Oh yeah?' said West, grinning. 'She hungry for you then?'

'Put it this way, Charlie, if music be the food of love, then that lassie's a walking juke box. How'd you get on?'

'Uniform are charging the taxi driver as we speak,' said West. 'His name's Tomek Dubrowski and we're doing him for vehicle theft, robbery and failing to report an ex-Norwegian. They're running some more checks too, see if he's got a record or anything.'

'Okay, good.'

'Plus, he's been working illegally, doing something very dodgy.'

'What do you mean?'

'Dunno yet, haven't figured it out but I reckon he's a runner of some sort,' said West handing Dougal the mobile phone, 'do me a favour, first number on the list, see if you can trace it please.'

'That's not as straightforward as you think, Miss.'

'I know, but it starts with 07789, that's Vodafone. Should narrow it down a bit. Oh, and get this, he's been having a wotsit with a woman by the name of MacAllister.'

'Am I missing something here?' said Munro. 'Is it illegal to fraternise with folk by the name of MacAllister now?'

'Could be,' said West, as she crunched her way through a sandwich. 'She's the manager of a restaurant where Dubrowski used to work.'

'And that's of interest, why?'

'It's Carducci's.'

'Are you serious?' said Dougal, handing out the tea.

'I know, blinding, isn't it? I think there might be something going on, you know, the pair of them bumping off the boss?'

'Aye, you may be right Charlie,' said Munro, 'but why? If I were you I'd have another word with this MacAllister lady and see what kind of relationship she has with her employers but now, more importantly, I've something else for you to chew over, courtesy of Miss McClure.'

'Don't tell me, she's asked you out!'

'That's as maybe,' said Munro, his face flushing, 'but I can assure you I'll not be making a deposit in her account anytime soon, that's for sure. Anyway, this Lars Gundersen, as we know, has an account with a branch of the DNB in Norway and last night his balance was boosted by the princely sum of fifty thousand pounds.'

'Fifty grand?' said West.

'That's right, Charlie. So you have to ask yourself the question: why? Why the sudden flurry of activity on the account when up until now it's been used as nothing more than somewhere to stash the cash?'

'Beats me,' said West. 'Where'd it come from? This fifty grand?'

'Answers on the back of postcard…' said Munro. 'Well come on, anyone?'

'Remus Trading?' said Dougal.

'Well done, laddie, award yourself a teacake.'

'We dinnae have any.'

'Shop's on the corner. Another thing: according to the bank, The Clydesdale that is, all correspondence relating to the Remus account is still being sent to Buchanan's address.'

'You what?' said West, slurping her tea. 'Buchanan?'

'Correct.'

'Well that means someone's not being entirely straight with us…'

'Correct again.'

'…and it could only be Heather Buchanan or Carducci. They're the only ones who could operate that account.'

'A hat-trick,' said Munro, folding his arms and smiling. 'So what are you going to do about it?'

West froze as though she'd just discovered the sausages she'd been eating were made from tofu.

'Me?' she said glaring at Munro, her face filled with trepidation. 'But I thought you were… I mean, we were both…'

'It's not my case, Charlie, you're the one in charge.'

'Right. Of course I am,' said West, attempting to assert herself. 'Okay, I think we should pay them a visit, Carducci and Buchanan. We need to take a good look around because obviously the letters from the bank have to be there somewhere.'

'Maybe,' said Munro. 'And maybe not.'

'Come again?'

'There may be a third party involved, albeit unwittingly.'

'Sorry, am I being stupid? We just agreed that…'

'Charlie. Remus is a limited company, lassie, as such…'

'I see where you're going, Boss,' said Dougal, butting in enthusiastically. 'If Remus is a limited company then they have to file returns at the end of the financial year so they must have an accountant.'

'Two teacakes for the boy.'

'Of course!' said West, 'So maybe the accountant's holding the statements. Genius. Right, I'm on it. I'll ask Carducci who it is. Dougal, we'll need a couple of warrants, one for Buchanan and one for Carducci, can you…'

Dougal reached across his desk, picked up two envelopes and waved them at West.

'I don't believe it,' she said looking at Munro as he gazed trance-like into space, a subtle frown furrowing his forehead, 'you're always one step ahead. How on earth do you… what is it?'

Munro, his mind elsewhere, took a deep breath and exhaled slowly as if lost in the midst of a deep meditation.

'Something Heather mentioned,' he said. 'It may just be a coincidence but as we've a dead body with a split personality I see no harm in following it up.'

'What the hell are you talking about?' said West.

'Oslo.'

'Oslo?'

'Capital of Norway,' said Dougal.

'Really? You astound me. What about it?'

'Heather mentioned that Mr Buchanan and Signor Carducci were there not so long ago on a wee golfing holiday,' said Munro.

'Are you kidding me?' said West. 'Golf? In Norway?'

'Oh aye, it's about as popular with Norwegians as cabbage rolls. Charlie, you take yourself off to Carducci's and have a nose around, ask him about their last golfing trip while you're there. I'm away to see Heather. Incidentally, just so you know, I'll not be mentioning anything about her husband, not just yet. I suggest you do the same.'

'Mum's the word. Dougal, fancy a ride in a Figaro?'

'If I knew what that meant, Miss, I might be tempted, but I've enough to do here.'

* * *

Remo Carducci – oblivious to the small foreign-looking car parking precariously close to the tail end of his Carrera – was lapping up the last of the afternoon sun, wandering lazily around the garden, half-heartedly pushing a lawnmower as Andrea Bocelli battered his eardrums through a pair of over-sized headphones. The sight of a lean-looking West, dressed in black jeans and a white tee shirt marching determinedly through the gate, her mobile phone hanging from her hip like a revolver, stopped him dead in his tracks.

'Hold on,' he said, smiling as he pulled off his headphones, 'don't tell me, I'll get it, it's… West? Sergeant West.'

'Afternoon, Mr Carducci. Mind if I have a word?'

'Remo, please. Is that Constable McCrae not with you today?'

'Nope.'

'Well in that case, will you take a glass of wine? I'm just about to have one myself.'

'No thanks,' said West, 'I just need to ask you a few questions.'

'As you wish. I assume it's Angus you've come about, any progress?'

'Nothing concrete I'm afraid but we're working on it. It's early days yet.'

'Of course it is,' said Remo, ruffling his mane of thick, black hair. 'Still, you can't help but worry. It's Heather I feel for, the poor woman's beside herself.'

'Well that's hardly surprising. Shall we go inside?'

* * *

Remo led them to the kitchen, uncorked a half-empty bottle of Barolo and filled a glass to the brim.

'Last chance,' he said, holding the glass aloft. 'I can't stand drinking alone.'

'You'll just have to force yourself,' said West, declining the offer. 'Your old company, Remus Trading…'

'Remus? That's going back a bit. How is that of interest?'

'Everything's of interest Mr Carducci.'

'Oh I get it, no stone unturned, eh?'

'Something like that. So, have you anything here relating to Remus? Any paperwork, invoices, bank statements?'

'No, no,' said Remo, 'that was Angus's side of things, I had nothing to do with it.'

'You're quite sure? Nothing you may have forgotten about, some files in your study or office maybe?'

'Office? I'm not Richard Branson, hen. Like I said, there's nothing here, you're better off talking to Heather, maybe she… oh hold on, come with me.'

West followed him through to the lounge where he ran a finger along a row of hardbacks lining the bookshelf before pulling out a brown envelope sandwiched between Aldo Zilli and Giorgio Locatelli.

'Here you go,' he said triumphantly, 'I almost forgot I had this.'

'What is it?' said West as she peered inside.

'If I remember correctly, it's a copy of the company registration document.'

'And that's it? Nothing else?'

'No. Nothing else.'

'Okay look, Mr Carducci, you should know I have warrant to search this place which I will, from top to bottom if I have to.'

Remo took a seat on the sofa, leaned back and crossed his legs.

'Feel free,' he said smiling broadly, 'I could even give you a hand if you like and if you get hungry I could rustle up some supper too. Are you fond of pasta?'

'Too many carbs,' said West, scowling. 'Now, if you don't mind I need to take a look at your computer, unless you're gonna force me to requisition it.'

Remo smiled and raised his eyebrows.

'You don't have a computer,' said West with a sigh.

'Afraid not. Anita has one of those tablet things but a mobile phone is as far as I'll go when it comes to embracing technology.'

'I see. Okay, how about your accountant? I don't suppose you happen to know who it is? Or is that Mr Buchanan's department too?'

'Ah, now that I can help you with,' said Remo, 'it's written on the back of that envelope. Ferguson's. They're on Wellington Square I think. Ask for a fella by the name of Kincaid, he's your man.'

'Thanks,' said West as she turned to leave, 'appreciate your time. One more thing before I go. Oslo.'

Carducci smiled and shook his head.

'What of it?' he said.

'You were there recently. With Mr Buchanan. Golf, wasn't it?'

'Aye it was,' said Remo, 'but it's not somewhere I'd recommend, not with the prices they charge. Especially for a pint. It's enough to make a man give up the booze completely. Either that or face bankruptcy.'

'But why Oslo? I mean, it's not the first place you'd think of when you mention golf.'

'That's precisely why,' said Remo, 'we fancied a change. Rubbing shoulders with ex-cons at the nineteenth on the *Costa del Cockney* was getting tedious. I've my eye on Greenland or the Himalayas for our next trip although I'm not sure Heather or Anita will take too kindly to us disappearing for a month or so.'

'Oh, I don't know,' said West with a smirk. 'You might be pleasantly surprised. I'll see myself out.'

'You know there's an old Italian proverb, Sergeant,' said Remo. 'Let every fox mind its own tail.'

'Meaning?'

'It means life is a little less complicated, and a lot more rewarding, if you keep your nose out of other folks business.'

'Is that a threat, Mr Carducci?'

'No, no. Just some friendly advice. That's all.'

* * *

West, having failed to negotiate the one way streets in the town centre despite the guidance of her sat-nav had given up, parked illegally and walked the five hundred yards to and from Wellington Square before returning to the office clutching a parking ticket, only to be greeted by Dougal and Munro looking about as happy as a pair of mourners attending the funeral of someone they neither knew nor cared about.

'Well if it isn't Grumpy and Sleepy,' she said, tossing her jacket on the desk and slumping in a chair, 'you two look as good as I feel. No luck then?'

'Not even a sniff,' said Munro, rubbing his eyes, 'according to Heather, Angus kept nothing at home. He was that efficient he'd bundle up all the paperwork and drop it off at the accountants every Friday, regular as clockwork.'

'Ferguson's? On Wellington Square?'

'Aye, that's them,' said Munro. 'How about you? By the look on your face I'm guessing your visit was just as fruitful.'

'And then some,' said West, crossing her legs on the desk. 'That Carducci makes my skin crawl, I never realised he was such a lech. Do you know he spent most of the time looking at my backside and flirting like he's God's gift to women?'

'The kind of gift you keep the receipt for?' said Munro.

'In one. You know what? I reckon the only person he's in love with is the ugly bloke he sees every time he looks in a mirror.'

'Which is quite often by the sounds of it.'

'And he doesn't even own a computer.'

'Ah, so he does have one redeeming feature after all,' said Munro sarcastically as he turned, hands clasped behind his back, to gaze from the window. 'Character analysis aside, I take it…'

'Yeah, zilch,' said West. 'There's nothing there. I even went to the accountant's office, that was another bloody waste of time. Waited ages for them to dig out the files only to be told the last dealings they had with Buchanan and Carducci were when they dissolved the company. Nothing since. At all. Ever.'

'You're awful quiet, Dougal,' said Munro, as he watched his own reflection in the window, 'something on your mind?'

'Aye. I mean, I just don't get it, Boss.'

'What don't you get?' said West, charmed his boyish state of confusion.

'Well, the Clydesdale, Miss. They're still sending letters to Buchanan's address, right? So unless the account's been hacked, which is highly unlikely, it's like you said, one of them, for some reason, has to be lying. I mean the post cannae just disappear.'

'Tell us something we don't know,' said West as she stood and rummaged through the cupboards. 'Got anything to drink?

'What do you think, Boss?' said Dougal.

'Drain cleaner will do.'

'I think, Dougal,' said Munro with a satisfied smile as he turned to face him. 'I think the mail is being re-directed.'

'I'll get some champagne.'

'Of course!' said Dougal, 'Dammit, it's obvious. If it's being re-directed then the bank wouldnae have a clue about it and either of those two could pick it up from wherever.'

'I was going to say that,' said West, 'got distracted.'

'Dougal, there must be a major Post Office hereabouts, you know, like a sorting office…'

'There is, Boswell Park.'

'Get on to them as soon as possible, find out where they're sending the post.'

'Will I go now?'

'Dougal, I appreciate you dinnae need much sleep. And I appreciate that, given half the chance, you'd prefer to work with a team of nocturnal mammals, but there's comes a point when you have to call it a day and right now I've an urge to dive headfirst into a bathful of Balvenie. So, that's us away then, let's…'

'Hold on, Boss,' said Dougal raising his hand as the chimes from his laptop heralded the arrival of a new email. 'It's from the Hordaland District Police, some news about

Lars Gundersen. Uh-oh. I'm not sure you're going to like this.'

'Come on, Dougal,' said West, 'I'm dying of thirst, what is it?'

'Lars Gundersen, Miss. The fella went missing two years ago. They've still not found a body.'

Chapter 9

Not one for languishing beneath the covers and cogitating on the day ahead, Munro – a habitual early-riser who ever since the untimely passing of his wife had sought solace in the chorus of blackbirds, robins and wrens as they foraged for food – sat sipping his second cup of tea in the cold light of dawn when a bleary-eyed West, her shoulders twitching against the frigid morning air, appeared on the balcony and sat bedside him.

'Blimey,' she said, yawning as she pulled her cardigan tight around her chest, 'did you actually go to bed or have you been up all night?'

'The early bird, Charlie.'

'What of it?'

'Gathers no moss. There's tea in the pot, will I fetch you a cup?'

'Yeah, thanks. No. In a minute.'

'Is something troubling you?' said Munro. 'Did you not sleep?'

'Just something that crossed my mind.'

'Think aloud, lassie.'

'Okay,' said West, 'but feel free to tell me if I'm being stupid.'

'I'll not need an invitation for that.'

'Buchanan. We're trying to figure out why he assumed the identity of a missing Norwegian bloke, right?'

'Correct.'

'So what if… what if it's the other way round? What if it's Lars Gundersen who's pretending to be Angus Buchanan?'

Munro, cradling the cup in both hands, stared pensively out across the river and took a moment before answering.

'Okay,' he said, 'so a Norwegian fellow comes ashore forty-odd years ago. Even if we assume he's fluent in English do you really think a gentleman with a Scandinavian accent could manage to pass himself off as a native Scot? Because that's what Mr Buchanan is.'

West's cheeks billowed with the weight of her sigh.

'Didn't quite think it through, did I?' she said.

'Perhaps you should. It's not entirely out of the realms of possibility.'

'How'd you mean?'

'Far-fetched as it may sound,' said Munro, frowning as he sought to justify the proposition, 'perhaps there *was* an Angus Buchanan. Perhaps this particular Angus Buchanan went to Norway as a wean with his family. And perhaps he died. That would lend credence to the theory that Gundersen's lack of a local accent was due to his being raised in Norway.'

'Of course!' said West. 'And he could've picked up the accent when he came here, I mean, he's been here long enough.'

'But why, Charlie? Why would a young Gundersen adopt a false identity?'

'Well, dunno yet. Because he did something bad? Maybe he had to leave the country?'

'Do you not think the Hordaland Police would have told us?'

'Oh yeah.'

'And why was he reported missing just two years ago and not twenty?'

'Think I'll get that tea.'

'And why have neither his wife or Carducci mentioned that Angus used to live abroad?'

'On second thoughts,' said West, 'maybe I'll just go back to bed.'

'You give up too easily, Charlie, but I'll give you this; it's good thinking. Inspired even. Aye, that's the word. Inspired.'

'Thanks. Obviously barking up the wrong tree though, aren't I?'

'Trust your instinct, lassie,' said Munro, 'it's the best tool you have. If you really think there's something in it, then start digging. A wee search of the census for any Angus Buchanans who emigrated around sixty years ago wouldn't go amiss.'

'Nah, you know what? It's not worth it,' said West as she reached for her phone, flinching at the missed call before retrieving a message. 'Text from Dougal.'

'Dougal? By jiminy, I told you the lad has the sleeping habits of a vampire.'

'You'll like this. That number I asked him to trace? The mystery man on Dubrowski's phone? Well, speak of the devil, it's Angus Buchanan.'

'Then it's time for another chat with Mr Dubrowski.'

* * *

PC Anderson – halfway through the early shift and thankful that, thus far, he'd not had cause to leave the office – was ambling back from the canteen carrying four cups of something the vending machine had told him was coffee when he caught sight of Munro and West breezing hurriedly through the lobby.

'Miss!' he called. 'DS West! Can I have a word?'

West stopped in her tracks and glanced at Munro.

'I'll catch you up,' she said, 'interview room, ten minutes, okay?'

'Sorry,' said Anderson as he sauntered casually towards her, 'dinnae mean to hold you up. I'll not keep you.'

'No trouble,' said West, 'what's up?'

Anderson, for no apparent reason, glanced over his shoulder and lowered his voice.

'There's a fella round front been asking for you,' he said.

'Me? Who on earth could be asking for me? I don't know anyone up here.'

'Well he says he knows you and he's not for moving. Thing is Miss, he's a wee bit… how can I put this politely? *Unsavoury.*'

West, amused and intrigued, smiled curiously.

'Don't suppose he has a name by any chance?'

'Aye,' said Anderson, 'Lyndhurst. Toby Lyndhurst.'

West, eyes wide with disbelief, gazed at Anderson as her smile wilted away and a sinking feeling in the pit of her stomach urged her towards the ladies.

'Shit,' she muttered under her breath, 'tell him… tell him I'm out on a shout or…'

'Right you are but like I say, he's not in a hurry to leave.'

'Okay,' said West, taking a deep breath, 'let's nip this in the bud. Where is he?'

'Reception. Are you okay? Will I come with you?'

'No thanks, I'll be fine. It's just some rubbish I thought I'd thrown out ages ago.'

Chapter 10

The malnourished individual scurrying around reception like a beetle on speed was not the Toby Lyndhurst West once knew. Gone was the charming, mild-mannered man who'd swept her off her feet. Gone was the sartorially elegant, blue-blooded male who'd promised her the earth. In his place stood a borderline vagrant, his clothes filthy and torn, his face an undulating landscape of blotches and blemishes, scabs and scars – a desperate down-and-out with little or no self-respect. She felt no sympathy. Not even a hint of compassion. Just an overwhelming sense of loathing and contempt.

As an adolescent growing up in the rural idyll of the rolling Sussex countryside, Tobias Lyndhurst – accomplished horse-rider and all-round animal lover – had harboured ambitions of becoming a botanist; then, as the years progressed, a veterinarian surgeon, a vocation he enjoyed with moderate success until finally, on the occasion of his thirtieth birthday, any desire he'd had to continue working for a living evaporated with the news that a trust fund set up in his name was ripe for the picking.

With a rugged physique honed on the rugby pitch, youthful good looks and a substantial inheritance in the offing, he was considered by many amongst the champagne-swilling set to be quite a catch. However, much to the chagrin of the fawning sycophants looking for somebody to sire their off-spring he opted instead – after a chance meeting with a young police officer at the Old Berkshire Hunt – to forsake them all, temporarily, for the comparatively modest and refreshingly down-to-earth Charlotte West, although later returning their advances throughout the entire nineteen months and twenty-three days of their doomed engagement.

* * *

'What the bloody hell are you doing here?' said West, trying her damnedest not to shout.

'Nice to see you too,' said Toby, his smile revealing rows of blackened teeth, 'I tried calling a couple of times but…'

'Outside now! I'm not having you hanging round here.'

'Charming. I come all this way to see you and all I get is abuse.'

'I haven't even started yet,' said West, glowering with rage. 'Last chance, what the bloody hell are you doing here?'

'Okay, okay. I was passing through and I thought I'd stop by and say…'

'Passing through, my arse. Where were you going?'

'Haven't decided yet,' said Toby, 'I'm not in the habit of making plans these days.'

'No change there, then. You could never stick to them anyway. Look at the state of you; you're pathetic. What is it? Heroin?'

'Does it matter?'

'Not to me,' said West, raising her hand as he moved towards her. 'That's far enough. How'd you find me?'

'Wasn't difficult, I asked around. Your old mates said you'd moved up here.'

'So you've followed me?'

'Of course not,' said Toby, scratching his head as though troubled by an indeterminable infestation, 'I told you, I just…'

'Shut it,' said West gritting her teeth. 'Just shut it. I'll tell you what's going on, shall I? You're here because you've got nowhere else to go. Because Daddy's cut off your allowance. That's it, isn't it? No more trust fund. Shame. My heart bleeds. And now the privileged little rich kid's got no-one to play with except winos and smackheads.'

'You've got it all wrong, Charlotte, honestly. Just hear me out. I've been missing you, okay? Look, I screwed up big time and now I realise just what a…'

'You make me sick. Get the hell out of here before…'

'Look,' said Toby, his mood growing increasingly angry, 'I just need somewhere to crash for a couple of nights until I get myself sorted, then I'll be on my way.'

'No bleedin' way. Now for the last time, do one.'

'Oh come on, just a few quid then, just so I can…'

'So you can what? Blow it on more shit? Do yourself a favour Toby, check into rehab, find a hostel or go back to one of the in-bred tarts you were so fond of, cos if I see you round here again so help me God I'll…'

'You'll what?' snarled Toby, his eyes narrowing as his mood became more threatening, 'Call for back up? Fat lot of good that will do you.'

'You're forgetting something you stuck-up scumbag, you're not in bloody Sussex now. You're in Scotland. And if I have to get my mates out here then trust me, they'll bloody well eat you alive. Now piss off.'

West, still seething, watched as he ambled through the car park randomly flicking wing mirrors along the way before stepping into a line of speeding traffic to the sound of screeching brakes and raising two fingers at the drivers who instantly regretted not mowing him down. She watched and waited until he'd disappeared from view before heaving a sigh of relief and bolting down the stairs towards the interview room.

* * *

Dubrowski, happy to answer any number of questions in return for the free accommodation and endless supply of hot meals on offer, regarded Munro with a look of trepidation as they sat opposite him.

'Alright?' said West curtly. 'This is Detective Inspector Munro.'

'You have a serious face,' said Dubrowski, 'I think you are like *the bad cop*, yes?'

'No,' said Munro, fixing him with a steely glare, 'I am like *the Beelzebub*.'

'Who is this Beastly Bob?'

'He's the gentlemen who'll be looking after you once you slip this mortal coil. Now, for your information, Mr Dubrowski, we know who the mystery man on your telephone is. The fellow you've been working for.'

'Then you are knowing more than me.'

'Not difficult,' said West, 'so, first question: the work you did for him, what did it entail exactly?'

'I am already saying this. I collect parcel, sometimes is a bag or suitcase, and I take it to address. Taxi drivers do this kind of work all the time. I think.'

'And what was in these bags or cases?'

'I am not knowing this. It's private property, it's not good manners to look inside.'

'That's rich coming from you,' said West with a sneer, 'considering the last bag left in your possession was found a few grand lighter. So. Where do you collect these parcels from? Is it always the same place?'

'Tak,' said Dubrowski, nodding, 'is always the same place. It's what you call a locker-up. A self-storage unit near to the ferry terminal. The other policemen have the key with my other belongings if you want to see it.'

Munro stood unexpectedly, checked his watch and, as though bored with the entire proceedings, clasped his hands behind his back and sighed as he began to slowly pace the periphery of the room.

'Tell me Mr Dubrowski,' he said, 'where exactly did you take these cases once you'd collected them? Did you drop them off at different locations? Different houses?'

'Nie, nie, is always to the same place. I know this address from memory, it is Dalblair Road. I leave bag inside door, wish them a good day and I go.'

'And was this regular work?' said West. 'I mean, once a week? Twice a month?'

'Nie, there is nothing regular about it, it's always different. I get message on my phone, sometimes in middle of night even. Sometimes he is sending me a text two or three times in one week, sometimes nothing and sometimes maybe there is just one trip in whole month.'

'And how much does he pay you? I'm guessing it's more than the regular taxi fare.'

'Very much more,' said Dubrowski with a satisfied grin, 'he is paying me two hundred pounds per trip.'

'I'm in the wrong line of work,' said Munro.

'And how does he pay you?' said West.

'Cash. Always he is paying cash. In envelope in locker-up with case.'

'Okay, hold it right there. Now, you need to get your story straight, Mr Dubrowski. Last time we spoke you told me you picked up your payment from a pub or a waste bin, so which is it?'

Dubrowski raised his hands.

'It's the locker-up.' he said.

'So why did you lie?'

'The man, he has been good to me. I do not want to get him into troubles.'

Munro stopped pacing, turned to face the back of Dubrowski's head and held his breath, allowing an ominous silence to fill the room.

'How did you meet?' he said quietly.

Dubrowski's shoulders rocked gently as if he were laughing to himself, as if he'd dodged a trick question.

'Your memory is maybe not so good,' he said, 'I am saying this to you already. I have never met this man.'

Munro walked silently across the room and leaned forward, close enough for Dubrowski to feel his breath on the back of his neck.

'Then let me re-phrase the question, Mr Dubrowski,' he said, 'before you're forced to answer any further questions from the comfort of a hospital bed. Who put you in touch with him?'

'It was… it was my girlfriend.'

'You don't have a girlfriend,' said West, tersely, 'you have sex occasionally with your ex-boss. Is that who you mean?'

'Tak.'

'Clare MacAllister?'

'Tak.'

'Go on.'

'She says to me I need the monies and she knows a man who needs parcels collected, will I do it? Of course, I says, thank you, thank you very much.'

West, distracted by the buzzing in her pocket, grabbed her phone, glanced at Munro and nodded towards the door.

* * *

'So,' said West as they thumped their way up the concrete steps to the office, 'what the hell was Buchanan up to? I mean, what was in those bags?'

'Your guess is as good as mine,' said Munro, 'but I'll tell you this for nothing: he didnae want to get caught with them. That's why he paid Dubrowski a substantial sum to cart them around.'

'You mean hush money, so he'd keep his mouth shut if ever he was caught?'

'Precisely,' said Munro, pausing on the landing, 'and whatever was in those bags came from abroad. Probably off the ferry.'

'Scandinavia?'

'Not necessarily. Could've come from anywhere in Europe or even farther afield. I'd say the ferry terminal was the path of least resistance.'

'Okay, so we're looking at smuggling then?' said West. 'Makes sense I suppose. Do you think Buchanan made the trips himself?'

'No, no. There's someone else involved. Think about it. Why pay Dubrowski two hundred pounds to avoid getting caught but run the risk of carrying the bags through customs? No. I think whoever was bringing the stuff over met Buchanan at the lock-up.'

'Maybe Dubrowski knows who it is.'

'Ask him,' said Munro as they entered the office, 'but be quick. We cannae hold him much longer, you need to charge him today. And have a chat with that MacAllister woman too, as soon as possible.'

'Will do,' said West, slumping in a chair as Munro reached for the kettle. 'So come on then, Dougal. What's so urgent that you had to buzz me in the middle of an interview?'

Dougal leaned back in his chair, folded his arms behind his head and smiled as if he'd just discovered the secret recipe for Irn-Bru.

'Merry Christmas,' he said grinning.

'Same to you,' said West. 'I hope you baked a cake cos I'm starving.'

'She's not the only one, laddie,' said Munro, 'and just for the record, I had a fried egg sandwich on my Christmas list.'

'No, no,' said Dougal, becoming flustered, 'when I said Merry Christmas I was speaking metaphorically, as in, I've made a breakthrough.'

'Shame.'

'Anti-climax,' said Munro, filling the mugs.

'It's about the Remus account. I know where the post is being re-directed.'

Munro turned to face Dougal, placed the index finger of his left hand on the bridge of his nose and spoke slowly.

'Dougal,' he said, 'look at me. Concentrate on the address and look directly into my eyes. Say nothing. Just concentrate on that address. Understand?'

'Aye,' said Dougal, bemused, 'okay. Concentrating now.'

Munro returned his stare with an unblinking gaze, held it for sixty seconds and sighed as though exhausted by the effort.

'Dalblair Road,' he snapped, plonking three mugs of tea on the desk.

'What? How the hell…? How could you possibly know the post was being sent to…?'

'Telepathy,' said Munro with a grin, 'so if I were you, I'd not think too hard about that lassie you've your eye on.'

'Crap.'

'Okay. I think it's time we had another a wee quiz. How are you on languages, laddie?'

'Not bad,' said Dougal, 'I speak one all the time.'

'Good. So if I said to you *baguette saucisse*, what would you say?'

'Sausage sandwich.'

'Good. *Bocadillo de jamon y queso*?'

'Ham and cheese sandwich.'

'Excellent. And finally: *Je vais aller au café maintenant*.'

'I'll go to the café now.'

'That's very kind of you, Dougal. Much appreciated. Here's a tenner, get something for yourself while you're at it.'

* * *

Munro sat down, loosened his tie and ran his fingers through his thinning grey hair, casting a sideways glance at West as he did so.

'What's up?' she said. 'Obviously something on your mind.'

'Condolences, Charlie,' said Munro.

'Excuse me?'

'Conveying them. It's the one thing I can never get my head round, playing the harbinger of doom.'

'What do you mean?'

'Heather Buchanan. It's time she knew what's happened. I cannae keep her in the dark any longer, besides, we need a positive ID on her dearly departed.'

'You know what you need?' said West. 'Cheering up. How about a couple of fillets, home-made chips and a decent bottle of Burgundy for dinner?'

'That sounds just the ticket,' boomed DCI Elliot as he barged through the door, 'am I invited?'

Munro looked up and smiled.

'George, this is a surprise,' he said.

'I could say the same thing, James. I thought you'd buggered off home a couple of days ago.'

'I wish I had. Tomorrow maybe, if I can tear myself away.'

'Dinnae be so hasty,' said Elliot, commandeering Dougal's mug of tea, 'these fellas could do with the benefit of your experience. No disrespect, Charlie, but staffing levels being what they are…'

'None taken,' said West, 'if you can convince him to stay then…'

'No, no,' said Munro, holding up his hands, 'you keep forgetting Charlie, I'm not a charity.'

'Come, come, James,' said Elliot with a wry grin, 'you're not telling me you want to be recompensed for your time, surely?'

'Are you joking me?'

'Och, you're enjoying yourself, I can tell. Besides, we both know what you're like once you get a wee sniff of something, you're like a terrier with a bone.'

'Aye, right enough but if that's the case I've a few items that need listing on an expenses form.'

'List away, James,' said Elliot as he placed the empty mug on the desk, 'and dinnae fret about materialistic things like money, I'll find a way around it. Right, that's me away then, thanks for the tea.'

'There you go,' said West as he left the room, 'things are on the up. Maybe you should ask for a rise.'

'I'm not sure retired officers are eligible, lassie,' said Munro as Dougal returned, 'in fact, I'm not sure they're even supposed to be working.'

'Okay, who's the bocadillo and who's the baguette?' said Dougal, a look on confusion on his face as he spied the empty mug.

'I'll take the ham and cheese,' said Munro, 'Charlie here needs the protein.'

'Very good,' said Dougal, 'so what's next?'

'Storage unit up by the ferry terminal. Keys are with Dubrowski's belongings. Take a look, will you? We're away to see Heather Buchanan just now, time she found out what happened to her husband.'

'Hold tight,' said West, taking an over-generous bite and wiping a dollop of brown sauce from the corner of her mouth, 'I have to make a call before we go.'

* * *

The afternoon sun, though not exactly tropical, was warm enough to draw a sizeable crowd of alfresco diners to Carducci's on Prestwick Cross where the die-hard traditionalists tucked into plates of square sausage, black pudding, eggs, bacon and tattie scones alongside those with a more adventurous palate who winced as they found the *pollo arrabiata* too spicy for their underdeveloped taste buds.

Clare MacAllister, whose management skills were limited to opening the café at seven a.m., cashing up at close of play and reserving the best table for "staff" sat supervising a latte, her face hidden by a pair of over-sized sunglasses like some forgotten actress dining out on "used-to-be" in the once fashionable Juan-les-Pins. She stubbed out her cigarette, tucked a tress of auburn hair behind her ear and answered the phone, holding it to her lips like a calorie-laden flapjack she was unsure about eating.

'Clare MacAllister,' she said brashly as if it were her agent offering her a career-reviving role, 'how can I help?'

'DS West. Alright to talk?'

'Well I am rather busy just now but go ahead.'

'It's about Mr Dubrowski.'

'Oh aye, Tomek. I expect he's been asking for me.'

'No. He hasn't.'

'Oh.'

'I understand you found him his last job,' said West, 'the one delivering parcels. Is that right?'

'In a manner of speaking.'

'What manner exactly?'

'Well it wasnae me who gave him the job, exactly,' said MacAllister, 'I was asked to find out if he'd be interested.'

'Who asked you?'

'Mr Buchanan,' said MacAllister.

'You're sure about that?'

'Oh aye. It was Mr Buchanan who asked me to find him a job here in the first place. Well, told me more like. And when I said I had to let him go because he didnae have his paperwork in order, he mentioned the courier job.'

'But why Tomek?' said West. 'I mean he must've known he doesn't own a car.'

'Right enough, but he's clever like that, Tomek. That's why he took the job with Kestrel, just so's he could get his hands on a motor.'

'And I don't suppose you happen to know how he and Mr Buchanan met?'

'No idea, but I do know Tomek used to drive for them,' said MacAllister, 'way back when, for him and Mr

Carducci I mean. They hired him to fetch stuff from Italy apparently, that's what he told me anyway, but that was years ago. I reckon Mr Buchanan has a wee soft spot for him because they've stayed in touch ever since.'

'And how often do you see Mr Buchanan?'

'Once in a blue moon, if that. He's not one for popping over if you know what I mean, that's more Mr Carducci's line.'

'He likes to keep an eye on the business?' said West.

'Carducci? The waitresses more like. He's an eye for the ladies, that one.'

'So you haven't seen Mr Buchanan recently then?'

'No,' said MacAllister, 'we just have a wee natter on the phone every now and then.'

'And the last time you spoke?'

'That'll be when he got me to ask Tomek if he wanted the courier job.'

'Okay, one more thing, Miss MacAllister; these parcels Mr Dubrowski picked up, any idea what was in them?'

'No idea, hen, and to be honest, I'm not really interested.'

* * *

Munro paused on the forecourt outside the office, zipped up his jacket and fumbled in his pocket for his car keys, frowning as he caught sight of a gangly, dishevelled miscreant lurking in the privet bounding the car park.

'Would you look at that?' he said, shaking his head. 'The bare-faced cheek of it, I mean, hanging around the police office of all places, has the man no shame?'

West gazed towards the hedge, swallowed hard and glanced furtively at Munro.

'Are you okay, Charlie?' he said. 'You seem pre-occupied, something bothering you?'

'No, I'm fine,' said West, forcing a smile. 'Actually, no. I'm not. It's my ex. He showed up earlier.'

'Showed up? Here? Dear, dear, dear. How on earth did he know you'd moved?'

'God knows. Asked around apparently.'

'I see. I assume you've spoken to him then?' said Munro. 'What's he after, some kind of reconciliation?'

'Nope. Hand-outs. Daddy's cut off his allowance and now he's skint and looking for somewhere to stay.'

'And he's hoping that you're the good Samaritan.'

'Something like that.'

'And are you?'

'You what?' said West incredulously. 'You mean let bygones be bygones after what he did to me? Come on, Jimbo, you know what a shit he is. He's bad news. He can fester for all I care.'

Munro drew a breath and solemnly shook his head.

'In all the time I've heard you speak of him,' he said, 'I never once realised things were that bad between you.'

'They weren't, I suppose,' said West, 'but things are different now. Let's just say he's developed a… problem.'

'Oh?'

'More of a habit actually.'

'I see. And would this habit be of the alcoholic variety?'

'And the rest.'

'I take it he's had a wasted journey then?'

'He's had a wasted life, Jimbo. If I ever see him again, it'll be too soon.'

'Well good for you, lassie,' said Munro. 'There comes a time when we all have to move on.'

'I thought I had.'

'You have, Charlie, which is why you'll not let this bother you. Just out of interest, where is he now?'

West lowered her face and spoke quietly into her collar.

'He's over there,' she said sheepishly. 'By the hedge.'

Munro, momentarily lost for words, stood open-mouthed, gawping at West.

'Him?' he said, flabbergasted. 'That's Toby Lyndhurst? Dear God, I'm not being funny, lassie, but when was the last time you had your eyes tested?'

West laughed quietly to herself.

'He never used to look like that,' she said, smiling, 'the bloke I was engaged to was actually quite good looking.'

'Has he been harassing you?'

'No, not really.'

'Not really?'

'He can be a bit… stubborn.'

'Does he know where you stay?' said Munro.

'No.'

'Okay, here. Take the keys and wait in the car.'

'But I was going to take mine,' said West.

'You listen to me, Charlie, if he sees your car and realises it's not Noddy behind the wheel you'll not remain a needle in the haystack for long.'

'Good point.'

'Now, on you go. I'll be along in a moment.'

* * *

Toby, noticing the figure striding casually across the car park was heading directly towards him considered beating a hasty retreat but, believing himself to be as invincible as a member of the House of Lords caught taking cocaine in a pole-dancing club, opted to stand his ground instead.

'Mr Lyndhurst?' said Munro, as he approached. 'Mr Toby Lyndhurst?'

'Who's asking?' said Toby, a cocky grin smeared across his face.

'I am. Munro's the name. James Munro.'

'Let me guess. Cop.'

'Correct. Mind if I have a wee word?'

'Actually, yeah I do. I haven't done anything wrong so why don't you piss off back to where you…'

'Trespassing,' said Munro. 'There's trespassing, loitering with intent, and vagrancy. I think that's enough to get us inside.'

'Yeah, right.'

'And once inside we'll take a wee look through your pockets, may even treat you to a cavity search if you're lucky and if we find anything…'

'Personal use, Plod. Can't do me for that.'

'Oh, but I can, laddie, and rest assured, if all I find is the tiniest, weeniest crumb, I will do you for intent to supply as well. Do I make myself clear?'

'God, you're boring,' said Toby. 'Anything else?'

'No, no, I think that's it. Oh, hold on, I almost forgot. Harassing a police officer.'

'Harassing a… you're the one who's… oh I get it! Charlotte, right? She's put you up to this, hasn't she?'

'No, no,' said Munro, 'I thought of it all by myself. I'm clever like that. So, here's the deal, you have two options. Option one gets you a roof over your head, a decent meal and an unlimited supply of nausea, vomiting, diarrhoea, muscle cramps, sweats and blinding headaches as you start to experience withdrawal symptoms from the junk you've been pumping into your body. Option two is the opportunity to walk away now.'

'Nah, don't think I fancy either of those,' said Toby as he pulled a crumpled cigarette butt from his pocket, 'think I'll just stay here for a bit. Wait for Charlotte.'

Munro took a single pace forward forcing Toby back into hedge, his arms flailing as he struggled to stay upright.

'See here, Mr Lyndhurst,' said Munro, gritting his teeth as he pulled him up by the collar, his cold blue eyes drilling menacingly into his, 'I'm not in the habit of repeating myself. I said. Start. Walking.'

* * *

Munro took the keys from West, fastened his seat belt and started the engine.

'He'll not be back,' he said matter of factly, a subtle smile raising one corner of his mouth.

'Oh God, please say you haven't threatened him with a trip to the ICU?'

'Me? Och, Charlie, I thought you knew me better than that. I just gave him some friendly advice, that's all.'

'Yeah, course you did, Jimbo. Course you did.'

Chapter 11

Throughout her entire forty-two-year marriage, Heather Buchanan had remained fiercely independent and enjoyed an active social life which normally involved consuming copious amounts of sponge cake washed down with endless cups of tea whilst Angus, being of a similar disposition, galavanted around Europe chasing golf balls across some distant fairway. However, without the security of knowing exactly where he was, who he was with and how to contact him, she was floundering in the void left by his absence. With no-one to cook for, no-one to clear up after and no-one to argue with, she was happy to embrace any distraction that came her way, even the sight of a police officer pulling up outside her front door.

'Good afternoon, Inspector,' she said with a welcoming smile, 'I see you've brought a friend.'

'Aye, this is Detective Sergeant West,' said Munro, 'she's leading the investigation into your husband's disappearance.'

'Well you're most welcome, the pair of you. Come along inside and make yourselves at home. Now, to what do I owe the pleasure? Are you standing in for social services or have you brought some news?'

'We have,' said Munro, 'but if it's okay with you, we've a couple of questions we'd like to ask first.'

'In that case I'll bring some refreshment, what can I get you?'

'I'll have a coffee please,' said West, 'if it's not too much trouble.'

'No trouble at all, dear. Inspector?'

'No, you're alright, thanks Heather. Is your friend Mrs Carducci not with you?'

'Not just now. Dare say I'll see her later, no doubt. Milk, sugar?'

'One sugar, thanks,' said West, calling to the kitchen. 'Mrs Buchanan, do you know if Angus knew anyone from Europe, anyone he might have stayed in touch with?'

Heather laughed as she returned with a mug of instant.

'Europe? Angus knew everyone from Europe, hen. What do you expect working on the docks?'

'Yeah, of course. But I mean, what about Scandinavia? Did he know anyone from say, Norway, for example?'

'Norway?'

'Aye,' said Munro, 'see Heather, we're just wondering if he was pals with a fellow by the name of Gundersen. Lars Gundersen.'

'Lars! Goodness me,' said Heather as if she'd just remembered she'd left the bath running, 'why yes, indeed. Och, he was such a good friend, I've often wondered what happened him.'

'Happened?' said West. 'How'd you mean?'

'Well, he just stopped coming round all of a sudden. I assumed he and Angus had had a falling out over something but Angus never mentioned it so I thought I'd just keep quiet, you know how it is.'

'So, this Lars Gundersen and your husband,' said Munro, 'they were good friends, would you say?'

'Oh aye, them and Remo. The three musketeers.'

'How did they meet?'

'On the docks of course,' said Heather. 'It was Lars who Angus and Remo hired to fetch the groceries from Italy.'

'But that was years ago,' said West.

'Aye, but Lars kept driving for them even when that stopped. I daren't ask why but you know Angus and Remo. Fingers and pies, right?'

'Right. So he was still around then?'

'He was,' said Heather, 'it was Lars who got them into golfing in Norway, the three of them used to go together.'

'Must have been expensive with all those flights and stuff,' said West.

'Somehow they always managed to get a deal. They even slummed it in the back of Lars's van a few times and travelled on one of the cargo ships.'

'Boys, eh?' said West. 'What are they like? Do you remember the last time you saw him? Lars? Just roughly.'

'Goodness me, now that is a question,' said Heather. 'Couple of years or thereabouts I'd say. Is it important?'

'Not sure yet,' said West, offering a reassuring smile. 'We'll see.'

'Well give him my best if you find him. So, Inspector, you said you had some news?'

'Aye,' said Munro clearing his throat, 'and I'm afraid it's not good.'

Heather looked him in the eye and paused as she bolstered herself.

'He's dead, isn't he?' she said, abruptly. 'Och, it's alright Inspector. To be perfectly honest, I've been expecting it.'

'You have?'

'I think so. Although hearing it now, you know, I'm not so sure.'

'Will I fetch you a drink? A brandy perhaps?'

'I think… yes. Thank you.'

'Thing is, Heather, we cannae be certain it's Angus. Not yet,' said Munro, handing her a glass. 'Would you be willing to view the body, to make a formal ID?'

'Of course, Inspector,' said Heather, downing her brandy. 'Of course. Is he far?'

'Glasgow. We'll run you there and back of course and if you like, you can bring a friend, Mrs Carducci perhaps? It's best to have some support at times like this.'

'Thank you, Inspector. That might be a comfort. When will we go?'

'Whenever you feel up to it. Tomorrow or the day after if that's not too soon.'

'No, no. Tomorrow will be fine.'

'Will you be okay?' said West, 'I mean, I can arrange for someone to come over and keep you company for a bit, if you like?'

'No, no. I think I'd prefer to be on my own just now. Besides, Anita will be along soon enough. I'll be fine. Honestly. Just fine.'

* * *

West, as green at dealing with bereavements as Munro was experienced, sat in silence and waited until they'd reached the end of Dalhowan Street before speaking.

'Tough old bird, isn't she?' she said, mournfully.

'Aye. But dinnae be deceived,' said Munro, 'she's not as hard as she seems. I can almost guarantee she's bawling into her handkerchief as we speak. And I'll not blame her for that.'

'She shouldn't be alone. Not at a time like this.'

'Folk have different ways of coping, Charlie. I'm sure she knows what's best for her.'

'Yeah, maybe,' said West, deflated. 'So, what shall we do now to cheer ourselves up?'

'I always find a good film never fails to lift the spirits,' said Munro, 'something like *Watership Down* perhaps.'

'Dalbair Road it is, then.'

* * *

Munro parked the car, slouched back in his seat and regarded the building opposite with a look of mild bewilderment.

'Are you sure this is it?' he said, frowning as he glanced up and down the street in search of a more suitable address.

'Yup. Positive,' said West.

'But a hair salon? And not just any salon mind, but one called "Ayr Raising". Doesnae inspire confidence in the establishment.'

'Could be worse,' said West.

'How on earth could it possibly be worse?'

'Could be called "Loch Tress".'

'Dear God.'

'Lunatic Fringe.'

'Have you finished?'

'Hair of the dog.'

'I'm going inside.'

* * *

The salon – either stuck in a time warp or cleverly designed to cater specifically for a more mature clientele – was an homage to the kitsch and glitz of a bygone era with gilt-framed mirrors, vinyl-upholstered chairs, hood hair dryers and a reception desk which looked more like a 1950s cocktail bar. The young girl barely visible behind it reluctantly closed her dog-eared copy of OK! Magazine, forced a smile and offered the kind of enthusiastic greeting normally reserved for customers who were hard of hearing.

'Hello,' she said, her head lilting to one side as if she'd broken her neck, 'I'm afraid we don't cater for gentlemen here, Sir.'

'I'm not here for a cut, Miss,' said Munro, 'I've little enough as it is and I'd rather hang on to it if that's okay with you.'

'We'd just like to ask you a few questions,' said West holding up her warrant card, 'won't take long.'

'Look,' said the receptionist, a mild look of fear creeping across her face, 'if this is about the lady who came in for highlights last week, it was an accident, honest. I think the stylist was just a wee bit heavy handed, that's all. It'll wash out, I'm sure.'

'Dinnae fret,' said Munro, amused, 'we'd just like to know who collects your post when you open for business of a morning.'

'Oh, I'm not here that early. I dinnae start until eleven.'

'So you've not seen any mail addressed to anyone other than this salon?'

'No. Sorry.'

'We understand you get a delivery here now and then,' said West, 'a parcel or a bag dropped off by a taxi driver? Kestrel Cars?'

'Oh aye, I know about that,' said the receptionist. 'Nice fella, very polite, foreign I think. Looks like his head's been through a mincer.'

'That's the chap. Do you know anything about him?'

'No, we dinnae say much. He just drops off the bag and that's him away.'

'Does it happen often?'

'No. I mean, yes. It depends. Sometimes he'll come by a couple of times a week then I'll maybe not see him for a month.'

'And have you any idea what exactly might be in these bags?' said Munro.

'No, I've not even been tempted to look. Too busy. Sorry, not much help am I?'

'You're being extremely helpful,' said West. 'What happens to the bags when they're dropped off?'

'I leave them here behind the desk and Annie picks them up whenever she comes by. I think she must know they're coming cos she's always here soon after.'

'I see. Annie, you say?'

'Aye, she's the owner.'

'Is she here just now?' said Munro. 'We'd like a wee word if that's possible.'

'No, she only pops in now and then. I imagine she'll show up in a day or two.'

'Okay, do you have a number where we can reach her?' said West.

'Aye, I'll write it down for you.'

'And you say her name's Annie. Annie…?'

'Annie… sorry, her full name's Anita. Anita Carducci.'

∗ ∗ ∗

Dressed in a pair of football shorts, flip-flops and tee shirt a size too small, Remo Carducci was obviously under the illusion that the village of Kirkmichael – soaking up what was left of the afternoon sunshine – was as warm as the eighteenth hole on the Santa Clara course in Marbella. Munro, wishing he could issue a fixed penalty notice for crimes against fashion, sneered as he watched him tip a bucket of soapy water over the Carrera and set about the bodywork with a chamois leather.

'Hello again,' said West as she slammed the car door shut.

'Why if it isn't the ever so lovely Sergeant West,' said Carducci, sarcastically. 'Have you come to rake up the past again? Oh, I see you've a chaperone with you.'

'This is Detective Inspector James Munro.'

'Inspector? Bringing out the big guns, eh?'

'This gun's about to be decommissioned,' said Munro, 'so have no fear, we'll not keep you long.'

'Take as long as you like.'

'Actually, it's Mrs Carducci we've come to see,' said West.

'Anita? And why's that?'

'We've reason to believe she may be…'

'We've reason to believe,' said Munro, interrupting, 'that is to say, we think her services would be much appreciated over at the Buchanan household.'

'You mean Heather?'

'Aye. She's a wee bit low at present, some company would do her good.'

'Dinnae fret on that score, Inspector,' said Carducci, 'Anita's good like that, she'll be heading over there later but truth be known, she's no substitute for Angus. Where are you with this investigation anyway? I mean, how hard can it be to find someone who's missing?'

'That all depends on where they're hiding,' said Munro.

'Aye, okay, I'll give you that. It's just that I'm missing the bugger, too.'

'I'm sure you are. Rest assured we're doing all we can but that's all I can say for now.'

'I understand.'

'So, your wife, Mr Carducci,' said West, 'any chance we could have a word?'

'Not just now, she's away up the shops fetching some bits and bobs for her trip.'

'Her trip?'

'Aye, she's away to see my papa. It's his ninetieth this weekend.'

'Good for him. Is it far?'

'About a thousand miles,' said Carducci. 'Avella. It's a nice wee place about a half-hour drive north of Naples.'

'And you're not going with her?'

'No, not just yet, I'll be leaving in a day or two, I've some business to sort out first.'

'Must be important,' said Munro. 'To keep you from your family, I mean.'

'A chain of restaurants willnae run themselves, Inspector. I have make sure everything's in order before I go.'

'I'm sure you do,' said West.

'Look, is there any chance we could see her before she goes?' said Munro.

'You seem awful keen considering it's just about Heather, Inspector. Are you keeping something from me?'

'No, no,' said Munro, 'just a few routine questions.'

'Is that so? Well, come by in the morning,' said Carducci, his shoulders twitching as the cold water took a hold, 'she's a flight to Stansted to get her connection but she'll not be leaving before ten I imagine.'

'We'll drop by then.'

'As you wish,' said Remo, 'oh, and Sergeant, remember what I said about the fox? it's worth bearing in mind, trust me.'

* * *

West watched from the corner of her eye as Munro, saying nothing, flicked down the visor against the setting sun, pushed back in his seat and headed in the direction of the office at a pace worthy of a pensioner on an excursion to the seaside.

'I was thinking,' she said quietly, 'why don't we just give her ring, Anita I mean? I've got her number now or better still we could just nip round to Buchanan's place and collar her there, it's not far.'

'Do you not think that's not a wee bit insensitive, Charlie? Heather's been through enough already. I'm not sure she'll appreciate us turning up and arresting her best friend on suspicion of aiding and abetting, wouldn't you say?'

'Yeah, suppose so,' said West. 'We'll have a word tomorrow, then.'

Munro gazed pensively along the road ahead and took a deep breath.

'What was all that nonsense about a fox?' he said.

'A veiled threat. It's the second time he's made it.'

'What kind of a threat?' said Munro.

'Friendly advice. About minding your own business.'

'So he was warning you off? Do you think he has something to hide?'

'Nah,' said West, 'to be perfectly honest I think he's got a cob on because I didn't succumb to his advances.'

'Okay, if you're sure that's all it is.'

'Positive,' said West. 'You think there's something else though, don't you?'

'Aye,' said Munro, 'it's just his…'

'His manner? I know. He seems too relaxed about the whole thing, like he doesn't really care about any of it. Is that what you were thinking, too?'

'No. Actually, I was thinking about his attire. For a man of his age it's nothing less than criminal. Aye, that's the word. Criminal.

* * *

Dougal McCrae, undoubtedly dedicated to his work and fanatical about fishing, was prone to the occasional bout of despondency over his inability to hook a female of the species who wouldn't baulk at the prospect of spending a rain-soaked weekend by the side of a loch with nothing but a book and a tin full of maggots for company, in the vain hope of landing a gargantuan trout before tossing it back and calling it fun.

Apart from a recent encounter with a lady thirty years his senior who threatened to devour him whole on the banks of The Doon, and without the necessary social skills to engage in idle tittle-tattle and a complete loathing of pubs and clubs, he resigned himself to the fact that, short of undergoing a lobotomy thus enabling him to enjoy football and the taste of lager, serendipity would have to play a major role in the acquisition of a soul-mate. Disgruntled at the lack of personal ads amongst the classifieds in Angling Times, he returned it to his bag as Munro and West returned to the office.

'Alright Dougal?' said West, tossing her coat on the table. 'Why the long face?'

'Och, no reason Miss. Probably just tired.'

'You've been overdoing it, laddie,' said Munro, 'what you need is a wee lassie to keep you company. That'll take your mind off work.'

'Tell me about it,' said Dougal, desperate to change the subject.

'Failing that, a decent brew is always a good substitute. Without the bromide.'

'I'll bear that in mind, Boss.'

'So, how'd you get on at the lock-up?' said West. 'Did you find anything interesting?'

'Nothing, Miss,' said Dougal, sighing with relief as he filled the kettle. 'Nada, zilch, zero. It was completely empty, nothing but space.'

'Pity. But it's Angus who rented it, right?'

'Aye. He's had it about a year and a half. The rent's paid by direct debit. No prizes for guessing which account it comes from.'

'Speaking of which, laddie, you'll be pleased to know the address on Dalblair Road where the mail is being forwarded to is a hairdressing salon owned by one Anita Carducci no less.'

'Anita Carducci? So she's the one who's kept the bank account going?'

'Possibly.'

'Possibly? It's obvious, is it not?'

'No,' said Munro, sipping his tea. 'She maybe just let Angus use the salon as somewhere to send the post.'

'But she'd have seen it was addressed to Remus Trading so surely Remo Carducci would've known about it? Would she not have told him?'

'Not if she and Angus were in cahoots over something,' said Munro. 'Something they didnae want Remo to know about.'

'This is getting awful murky, Boss,' said Dougal, 'So what happens now? Are you not bringing her in?'

'Yeah, course we are,' said West, 'in the morning. She's keeping Mrs Buchanan company at the moment so it's not a good time.'

'Okay, makes sense.'

'Meanwhile,' said Munro, draining his cup, 'as you've no diversions in the form of female company…'

'Thanks for reminding me.'

'…here's your next task: Dubrowski. He's been working for Angus and Remo Carducci for a couple of years, right? However, he took over the role from someone else. Guess who.'

'Absolutely no idea.'

'Lars Gundersen.'

'Lars Gundersen? Are you joking me?'

'I kid you not. So we need to find out what Dubrowski was up to before he came here, what he did for a living, where he lived. Got that?'

'Aye, Boss. I'll get on to it right away.'

'Dougal, Dougal, Dougal. Have you not seen the time? Tomorrow, laddie, tomorrow. You need to get some rest.'

Chapter 12

West pulled two fillet steaks and a packet of "twice-cooked-basted-in-goose-fat chips" from the fridge, plonked them on the counter and settled down at the dining table where she fired up her laptop as Munro, keen to sate a raging thirst, poured two glasses of Burgundy and a large Balvenie.

'Here you go Charlie,' he said, eyeing the box on the counter as he passed her the wine. 'Did you not say home-made chips when you mentioned dinner?'

'That's what it says on the packet,' said West.

Munro smiled mischievously.

'Have you booked yourself a holiday yet?' he said.

'Holiday? Bit of an odd question, no. Why?'

'I think you might find a week or two on the Costa Cordon Bleu beneficial.'

'And you might find a hotel beneficial if you don't want to be stabbed through the heart with a potato peeler. Stick the oven on, chips'll take a while.'

'Right you are.'

'Tell me something, Jimbo, don't you ever tire of eating steak?'

'Aye, I do,' said Munro. 'Occasionally.'

'Good, I'll cook something different tomorrow. What do you like when you're not eating steak?'

'Beef.'

'I give up,' said West with a smirk as the emails rolled in. 'Hup, you'd better sit down, I've got an email from Dougal. It's the results of the post-mortem on Angus Buchanan.'

Munro pulled up a chair, took a large glug of wine and leaned back, closing his eyes.

'You read, I'll listen,' he said. 'It'll be like Book at Bedtime.'

West sat with her elbows on the table, cradling the glass in both hands and frowned as she scanned through the report.

'Bloody hell,' she said, 'you couldn't make this up.'

'Go on.'

'Okay, cause of death was asphyxiation. He choked to death.'

'Choked to death?' said Munro. 'The poor man looked as though he'd seen the four horsemen of the apocalypse when we found him, are you sure?'

'That's what it says here,' said West. 'Hold on though, you were right after all. He did have a stroke, it's what he choked on that caused it.'

'I get the distinct feeling it's not a peppermint, is it?'

'Close. They found a sizable chunk of methamphetamine lodged in his throat.'

Munro opened his eyes, took another glug of wine and stood to check the temperature of the oven.

'Methamphetamine?' he said, his face crumpled with consternation 'You mean…?'

'Crank, Glass, Chalk, Ice,' said West, offering up her glass for a refill. 'Crystal Meth to you and me.'

Munro charged their glasses for a second time and leaned back against the counter.

'No, no. That doesnae fit,' he said. 'Angus Buchanan was not a user.'

'Acute overdose which brought about a stroke and heart attack.'

'Then it was administered,' said Munro. 'I'll stake my reputation on it. Somebody forced it down his gullet.'

'Only one person could've done that,' said West. 'Dubrowski.'

'Unless he was dead before they put him in the taxi.'

'Something else,' said West, 'they found traces of blood in his mouth…'

'Not surprising.'

'…thing is, it's not his. DNA test says origin unknown. There's no match on the database. They reckon he probably bit his assailant at some point while they were shoving it down his neck.'

'Okay, send a wee message to young Dougal,' said Munro. 'We need a DNA swab from Dubrowski, test for a match against the sample taken from Buchanan and we need a medical examiner to check his fingers for cuts and bites as soon as possible. Got that?'

'No probs,' said West, 'what are you going to do?'

'I'm going to put the chips in the oven.'

* * *

Munro, preferring his steak as tough as the sole of a well-worn shoe, tossed the fillets into the frying pan and contemplated a Balvenie as West set about laying the table, momentarily distracted by the ringing of her phone.

'Dougal,' she said, 'I just emailed you.'

'Aye, Miss. All sorted.'

'Hold on, I'll put you on speaker. Sorry, go on.'

'Okay, just to let you know I'll get that swab off Dubrowski before I leave and…'

'Hold on,' said Munro, 'sorry to butt in, Dougal, but are you still at work?'

'Aye, Boss.'

'I thought you were going home?'

'Aye, but you know how it is. I wanted to get a few things out of the way first.'

'If you're not careful, laddie, you'll catch yourself a vitamin D deficiency. You need to get out more.'

'I'm working on it. Anyway, as I was saying, I'll get that swab before I go and a medic will be here first thing in the morning to examine him.'

'Excellent,' said West. 'Nice one Dougal.'

'Nae bother, Miss, but the real reason I called is we've got the results of the background check on Dubrowski.'

'Go on.'

'It seems he's never held down a proper job, ever. No record of employment anywhere.'

'Okay, so nothing exciting then?'

'No,' said Dougal, 'apart from the fact he spent nearly seven years at the Gaustad Hospital in Oslo.'

'What's so exciting about that?' said West.

'It's a psychiatric hospital, Miss. He was admitted because of his suicidal tendencies.'

'No way?'

'Aye, apparently he was into self-harming, too. The reason his face is such a mess is because he decided to wash it with bleach. He'd been hallucinating after the doctors pumped him full of some drug they were trialling.'

'Well, bugger me. Poor sod.'

'And that's not all,' said Dougal. 'I found something odd, too. His last known address is Loddefjord.'

'And why is that odd?'

'Because Charlie,' said Munro, 'Loddefjord is the same place Lars Gundersen lived.'

'It's not just the same place, Boss,' said Dougal. 'It's the same apartment.'

Chapter 13

Cereal, mused Munro – in particular anything described as muesli – was fodder for hens and squirrels and should never under any circumstances be doused in milk and served as fit for human consumption when two soft-boiled eggs accompanied by a round of toast cut into soldiers provided a more palatable alternative.

He cringed as West, looking as though she'd just drunk a half a pint of castor oil, slammed the bowl on the table and grimaced with disgust.

'That was foul,' she said, coveting Munro's eggs. 'You having both of those?'

'If you want one, it'll take you precisely three minutes to prepare,' said Munro as he pulled his phone from his pocket, 'but you'll learn that on your first day at cookery school I expect. Excuse me while I take this.'

'Munro,' he said as West filched a piece of toast from his plate, 'who is this please?'

'Inspector. You've obviously not had time to save my number, have you?'

'Morning, Miss McClure. And what can I do for you at this Godforsaken hour?'

'I thought I'd catch you before your schedule prohibited you from taking any calls.'

'Schedule?' said Munro. 'I dinnae have a schedule, Miss McClure. I have palpitations. What is it?'

'The Remus account. If you check your inbox…'

'Sorry, I dinnae have an inbox either.'

'…if your colleagues check their inbox you'll find there's been another transfer on the Remus account.'

'Is that so?'

'Indeed. Last night. Another Cinderella transaction at one minute to midnight.'

'Cinderella? Very good, Miss McClure. Very good indeed. I assume the cash went into Gundersen's account in Norway?'

'Correct,' said McClure. 'Thirty thousand to be precise.'

'Good grief,' said Munro, exasperated. 'I'm not even sure my house is worth that. I appreciate the call, Miss McClure, really I do.'

'The pleasure's all mine, Inspector, but can I say one thing: there's really no need to be so formal. My name's Margaret as well you know.'

'Right you are. Margaret. Well I need to get on now so if it's all the same with you…'

'By the by,' said McClure, 'before you go, *James*, I've been offered a couple of tickets to a film next week. I don't suppose by any chance you're a fan of the silver screen?'

'No, not me,' said Munro, 'in fact I can think of nothing worse than sitting in a darkened room for ninety minutes with folk intent on filling their faces with over-priced snacks but thanks for the offer.'

'Pity. It's a night of vintage classics.'

'I really must…'

'High Noon, The Big Country and The Magnificent Seven.'

'Is that so? High Noon you say? Well, perhaps I'll get back to you. We'll see.'

* * *

Munro hung up, eyed his plate and stared at West in disbelief.

'Charlie,' he said, taking a sip of tea, 'something I need you to look in to.'

'What's that?'

'The case of the disappearing egg.'

'You were yakking so much it was going cold. I'll do you another. So, what did McClure want?'

'To throw a saddle on my back by the sounds of it.'

'Well that's great!' said West with a childish grin. 'You should go for it.'

'I'm a widower, lassie, not a bachelor. And when I took my vows I promised "until death us do part". And I'm not dead yet.'

'You're one of a kind, you know that?'

'Let's change the subject,' said Munro. 'There's been another transfer on the Remus account.'

'What? When?'

'Last night.'

'So hold on,' said West, 'if it was last night then that means it can't have been Angus Buchanan moving the money around.'

'No, no,' said Munro, 'it simply means someone else might have access to the account. You best get hold of Dougal while I see to the rest of my breakfast.'

West put her phone on speaker as Munro dropped an egg into a bubbling pan, popped a couple of slices into the toaster, stood back and checked his watch.

'Dougal,' she said, 'you sound like you're in a wind tunnel.'

'Aye, it's a wee bit breezy, Miss. What's up?'

'Someone's stuck another wedge of cash into that DNB account. We need to know if it's still there and if not, where it's gone. And while you're at it, find out if there's any other authorised signatories apart from Lars Gundersen.'

'Aye okay,' said Dougal. 'I'll do it as soon as I get to the office.'

'Do you mean to say you're not there yet?' said Munro, plucking his egg from the pan. 'What happened laddie, did you accidentally fall asleep?'

'No. I've been collared by DCI Elliot, Boss. Sounds like someone's had one too many up on the promenade. I'll not be long.'

'Okay listen, we're away to Carducci's just now. Call us when you're back.'

* * *

West, incapable of ringing a doorbell once and waiting politely for a reply, pressed it repeatedly, rattled the letterbox and hammered the door with the side of her fist like an irate bailiff on his fourth attempt at seizing goods to the value of an outstanding debt.

'It's not that early, is it?' said Munro.

'Seven-fifteen,' said West, 'anyone with a breath in their body should be up by now.'

Remo Carducci, wearing a dressing gown and an expression suggesting a night of over-indulgence, opened the door and winced as the sunlight burned his eyes.

'Dear, dear, dear,' said Munro, 'no offence Mr Carducci but are you familiar with a phrase involving the words "hedge" and "backwards"?'

'I wrote it, Inspector,' said Carducci, rubbing the side of his head. 'Come inside.'

'Late night, was it?' said West, smiling.

'When you get to my age hen, anything after nine o'clock is late.'

'I can vouch for that,' said Munro.

'Anita wasnae due back until nine so I nipped out for a wee bevy. You know how it is.'

'Not the first time, I'm sure.'

116

'No, but it might be the last. If there's a sure-fire way of upsetting your wife, Inspector, it's rolling in at one a.m. in a state of inebriation. Anyway, what brings you here? Not a Police Scotland alarm call, is it?'

'The alcohol's obviously had a detrimental effect on your memory, Mr Carducci,' said Munro. 'We're here to see your wife, remember? Anita?'

'Oh Christ, that's right. Well I'm sorry but you've missed her, and just as well, she was in a foul mood I can tell you.'

'Hold on,' said West, 'what do you mean missed her? Yesterday you said she'd be here until ten.'

'Did I? My mistake,' said Carducci, flopping down on the sofa, 'I must've got the times wrong.'

'When did she leave?'

'Och, now you're asking. Not too long, a half an hour maybe.'

'And she's going to Stansted?'

'Aye, from Glasgow. Then a connecting flight to Naples.'

Munro reached for his car keys and turned to West.

'Domestic flight,' he said, checking his watch, 'hour and a half check in and an hour to get there. We've plenty of time. Mr Carducci, which airline is she flying with?'

'Ryanair I think. No, no. BA. No, Ryanair'

'You're sure now, because we dinnae have time to…'

'Aye, quite sure. Ryanair.'

'Right, before we go,' said West, 'you mentioned your wife has a laptop or an iPad, is that right?'

'Aye. No laptop, just an iPad.'

'Would she have taken it with her?'

Carducci frowned as he glanced around the room and pointed to the bookshelves.

'No, no. It's there look, on the side.'

'We need to borrow it, okay?'

'Borrow it?' said Carducci. 'You can't just confiscate personal belongings on a whim, lassie. Do you not need a warrant or something?'

'All depends if you're in the mood for co-operating, Mr Carducci,' said West. 'If you're not, I suggest you grab your coat and we'll drop you at the station on the way. It's up to you.'

'No thanks, the only place I'm going is back to bed. You're welcome to it.'

* * *

The petulant passenger at the head of the queue, clearly disgruntled by the unexpected delay, raised his eyes to the heavens as West and Munro ushered him to one side and approached the girl behind the check-in desk.

'Morning,' said West as she flashed her warrant card, 'we need to know whether a passenger booked on your next flight to Stansted has checked in yet.'

'But… but this is for Dublin,' said the girl, flustered by the impromptu interruption.

'I dinnae care if it's for Timbuktu, Miss,' said Munro with a menacing smile, 'it's the Stansted flight we're interested in.'

'But that left ages ago.'

'Come again?' said West.

'Ten to seven. The Stansted flight left at ten to seven.'

'Well there's no way she'd have made that,' said Munro rhetorically. 'When's the next flight?'

'To Stansted?' said the girl. 'Not until this evening. About 5.45, I think.'

'Can you check the passenger list for that please. We're looking for a Mrs Carducci.'

'I'll try,' said the girl, panicking under pressure as she tapped away at the keyboard, 'I'm not quite sure how to… oh here we are. It's Carducci you say? And how are you spelling that?'

'Car. As in car,' said Munro tersely, 'then…'

'No, there's nothing beginning with car at all. We've a Corcoran if that's any good.'

'No, no. That will only result in a wrongful arrest. Just a minute, is there a Buchanan or a Gundersen perhaps?'

The young girl bit her bottom lip as she squinted at the screen.

'No, I'm afraid not.'

'By jiminy,' said Munro, 'this is intolerable. Okay listen, who else flies to Stansted from here?'

'EasyJet, I think.'

'Thanking you. Charlie, get Carducci out of bed and double check the details, he's so blootered I'll not be surprised if she's flying from Edinburgh instead. Then call Anita, see if she picks up.'

'Anita? Are you sure?' said West. 'Won't that scare her off?'

'She doesnae have your number, lassie. She's no idea who you are. Give her a call, I'm away to check with EasyJet.'

* * *

Munro, standing with his hands clasped behind his back, glowered at the sea of people milling around the check-in hall, instilling them all with an unwarranted sense of guilt as he waited for West.

'He's adamant,' she said as she sidled up beside him, 'Ryanair. This morning.'

'Then she lied,' said Munro.

'She's not answering either. It's going straight to voicemail. How'd you get on?'

'Nothing,' said Munro, sighing as he stared pensively into space, 'she's not booked with them either, she must have another…'

Munro's words tailed off as he turned to face West and slapped her on the shoulder.

'Ow!' she said, 'steady on. What's that for?'

'She's not flying to Stansted, Charlie,' said Munro excitedly, 'she's not even going to Naples. She's taking the ferry. She's away to meet Angus in Loddefjord.'

Chapter 14

For those arriving at the Ocean Ferry Terminal – invariably tourists who'd spent a week at sea trapped aboard a leviathan of a cruise ship – the warm welcome from the tartan-clad band of pipers parading up and down the quayside as they disembarked provided a myriad of photo-opportunities which undoubtedly made their inaugural visit to the shores of Caledonia a memorable one. For those departing, however, the quay was about as memorable and as inviting as an uninhabited retail park after dark.

Munro, cursing at the thought of having to do battle with hundreds of passengers, slew the car to a halt alongside the terminal building and dashed indoors only to find it as empty as an abandoned aircraft hangar.

'Dear, dear, dear,' he said, spinning on his heels, 'this is not what I expected. Not what I expected at all.'

'Nor me,' said West, 'I really thought you'd nailed it.'

An elderly gentleman with a shock of white hair, smartly attired in a blue blazer and matching trousers, emerged from the gents, waved in their direction and strode towards the information desk.

'Excuse me,' said Munro as he scurried after him, 'do you work here?'

'Indeed I do, sir. Tourist Board. Is there anything I can help you with?'

'Aye, as a matter of fact there is. Have you any boats departing today?'

'I'm afraid not,' said the old man, 'but we do have a ship.'

'Listen, if it floats and it carries people, that'll do for me. Where's it going?'

'Norway. It's called The Boudicca if you're interested.'

'I'll have it tattooed on my arm. Tell me, when does it leave?'

'She sails this evening, sir. Check-in is any time after two o'clock.'

'Would you happen to have a passenger list to hand?' said Munro.

'No, no. You'd have to speak with the tour operator about that. Someone normally arrives about an hour before check-in opens.'

'An hour? By jiminy, it's not even nine o'clock. Och, never mind, and… apologies for being so… abrupt. We've a wee crisis on our hands.'

'Not a bother, sir. I believe a cup of tea may help to calm your nerves.'

'Aye. So would something else.'

Munro, hands in pockets, strolled outside and gazed despondently out across the quay.

'Doesn't make sense,' said West, 'if you're right and she is booked on that ferry then why did she leave so early?'

'Because she's not stupid,' said Munro. 'She's orchestrated her departure to coincide with the flight times. Probably in case Remo checks up on her.'

'Still doesn't make sense,' said West. 'I mean he'll find out anyway when she doesn't show up in Naples.'

'Aye, right enough but by then it'll be too late.'

West leaned against the wall and, for want of something better to do, checked her phone for messages.

'If I smoked,' she said, 'now would be the ideal time to have a cigarette. Is there anything to do around here?'

'Not much but the town centre's only a five-minute walk away, why?'

'No reason, just wondering what she'd do for the next six hours while she's waiting to go aboard.'

'Who knows,' said Munro, 'shopping perhaps? Or maybe she'll have herself some breakfast and take a wee wander.'

'Or maybe,' said West, tapping him on the arm and pointing to a lone figure sitting on a bench in the distance, 'or maybe she'll just sit and read a book.'

* * *

'Mrs Carducci?' said Munro. 'Anita Carducci?'

'Who's asking?'

'Detective Inspector Munro. And this is DS West.'

'Not me,' said Anita, her chin nestling in the fur collar of her leather coat, 'I suggest you have a look in the departure lounge.'

'I've a feeling that won't be necessary. Mind if we join you?'

'Sorry, three's a crowd so if it's all the same with you, I'm away indoors'

'Sit down, Mrs Carducci,' said Munro sternly. 'A few moments of your time is all we need. A friendly wee chat.'

Anita pushed her book into her bag, sat back and folded her arms.

'So,' she said with a huff, 'what's this all about? Has Remo sent you?'

'Remo?' said West. 'Now why would Remo send us?'

'Because he… doesn't matter.'

'Not the best place to sit and read a book, is it, Mrs Carducci?' said Munro.

'It's peaceful,' said Anita.

'So is Crosshill. I expect you're looking forward to your trip?'

'Trip?'

'Aye, the cruise you've booked. I hear Norway has some spectacular scenery now of year. No doubt you'll be going ashore when you reach Bergen, visiting family perhaps. Or maybe you've booked yourself a nice wee hotel.'

'Don't be silly, Jimbo,' said West playfully, 'you're forgetting Mrs Carducci won't need a hotel, she'll be staying with her friend in Loddefjord.'

'Of course you will,' said Munro, slapping his thigh. 'Silly of me to forget. Tell me, Mrs Carducci, your husband Remo, does he know Mr Buchanan is still using the Remus bank account?'

Anita shivered against the breeze blowing in off the sea and swivelled uncomfortably in her seat.

'Remus?' she said defensively. 'Och, that was closed down years ago.'

'Was it really?' said Munro sounding surprised. 'It's a pity nobody told the bank then. It appears they're still sending out correspondence addressed to Mr Buchanan…'

'Is that so?'

'… aye. Only it's being redirected. To your hair salon.'

'Look, that's nothing to do with me okay?' said Anita, nervously. 'I swear, I was just doing him a favour. He asked me if I'd...'

'You'd best come with us, Mrs Carducci,' said Munro, 'there's no point in staying here. I do believe your ship has sailed.'

* * *

With Dougal out on a shout and no sign of the effervescent DCI Elliot – no doubt doubled over a desk struggling to fill rotas with the minimum of staff – the office, not exactly a hive of activity at the best of times, was as still as the deck of the Marie Celeste.

West threw her coat across the back of a chair and sat with her feet on the table as Munro, bemoaning the lack of anything edible in the cupboards, filled the kettle.

'I need a breather before we question her, Charlie,' he said, loosening his tie, 'let's have a wee brew.'

'Good idea,' said West, 'give her a chance to calm down.'

'The words "quivering" and "wreck" spring to mind.'

'Didn't seem too happy with the accommodation either.'

'She'll have plenty of time to get used it,' said Munro as he set the mugs on the table, 'if I'm not mistaken she's looking at three to five already for aiding and abetting and receiving stolen property, perhaps.'

'The letters from the bank,' said West as she sipped her tea, 'do you think she kept them at the salon?'

'If she's any sense, she'd have shredded them,' said Munro, 'but we should get a warrant anyway. Ask young Dougal to sort one out. Speaking of whom, have you not heard from him yet?'

'Not a peep,' said West.

'He's probably angling for a date with some minnow in a Tyvek suit.

'Leave him alone! Shall I give him a bell?'

'Aye, why not. It's nearly lunchtime, he could fetch some food on the way. Oh and ask him to drop by Heather Buchanan's, see when she's free for a trip to the morgue.'

* * *

Dougal, peeved by the interruption to his daily schedule and keen to return to his desk, stood on the promenade and watched as the SOCOs fastidiously combed the body for clues other than the blindingly obvious. He glanced at Mick – another junkie who claimed to have befriended the deceased less than twenty-four hours earlier – and smiled half-heartedly as he took the call.

'Miss,' he said, hoping she was calling with an urgent assignment, 'sorry, I'm still waiting for the overalls to finish up.'

'No worries,' said West, 'what've you got? Some drunk who's had seven shades knocked out of him?'

'I wish it was that easy, Miss. He's a druggie. Overdose by the looks of it, I'm with the fella who was with him when he died.'

'Well, I don't envy you,' said West, 'there's nothing more infuriating than trying to identify some no-mark without a single…'

'Och, that's the easy part, Miss. We know who he is alright, unless he pilfered someone's wallet.'

'Oh well, there you go…'

'Fella by the name of Lyndhurst. Mick says he was…'

'Hold on!' said West, 'Did you say Lyndhurst? Tobias Lyndhurst?'

'Aye, that's what it says on his driving licence.'

'Don't go anywhere. We're coming over.'

* * *

Having never lost anyone she considered to be "close" – apart from Archie, the beloved family dog who'd died at the ripe old age of fourteen – bereavement of a personal nature was something of a stranger to West. She sat staring at the privacy screens billowing in the breeze and took a deep breath, trying valiantly to keep her emotions in check as Munro, who'd learned from experience that space and time were not the exclusive domain of quantum physicists but essential ingredients in the grieving process, sat silently beside her.

'You don't mind doing this, do you?' she said quietly. 'I know it's taking our eyes off the prize but…'

'It's not up to me, lassie,' said Munro softly, 'the question is: are you up to it? If you'd rather, we can turn around right now and head back to the office.'

'No. I'm fine. I need to do it,' said West. 'Besides, if I can make a positive ID it'll speed things up which means we get Dougal back.'

'Okay Charlie, if you're sure,' said Munro as he unfastened his seat belt. 'Let's get this over with.'

Dougal, sporting a look of relief as if the cavalry had arrived, waved enthusiastically as West and Munro walked solemnly towards him.

'Miss. Boss. This is Mick,' he said. 'He was with the other fella when he died.'

Mick – his gaunt face protruding from beneath his charity-shop parka the only indication that he was severely underweight – was an ardent fan of any substance that could shut the door on reality and make the hunger pangs go away for a few hours at least. His ravaged face erupted in a sea of crinkles as he revealed a toothless but endearing smile and proffered a bony hand.

'Alright?' he said excitedly, 'this is some show, eh? Fascinating!'

'Fascinating?' said Munro, mildly amused.

'Aye! Those lads down there in the white suits, picking and plucking with their tweezers and their brushes, I've not seen anything like it in my life.'

'You're kidding,' said West, 'don't you ever watch telly?'

'Do I look like I have a telly?'

'Sorry. I wasn't thinking.'

'Nae bother.'

'Listen, do you have to be somewhere or would you mind hanging on for a bit.'

'No, you're alright,' said Mick cheerily, 'as it happens my diary's clear all afternoon.'

West, not knowing what to expect, glanced at Munro and stepped cautiously around the screens, drawing a breath at the sight of Toby lying flat on his back, his face somehow distorted, as if it had been pulled out of shape.

'That's him,' she said. 'That's Tobias Lyndhurst.'

Munro scrutinised the body: the pained expression; the bloodshot eyes; the left arm rigid by its side and the hand frozen like a claw.

'I'm sorry, Charlie,' he said, shaking his head. 'It's not a pretty sight. Are you okay?'

'Yeah,' said West with sigh, 'I'm okay. Stupid sod.'

'You're not upset?'

'Oddly, no. Not that much. Is that callous of me?'

'No.'

'Look, I know he didn't deserve to die but just for the record, he was a selfish two-timing bastard and he treated me like shit.'

'You dinnae have to justify your feelings to me, lassie,' said Munro, 'I understand completely. What about his family? Do you want to…?

'Oh no, no, no!' said West. 'No way. He may be my ex but that was years ago. I'm not getting involved. Count me out.'

'Probably for the best. Tell me, Charlie, do you notice anything familiar about him?'

'Are you having a laugh? Of course, everything.'

'No, no. I meant… look at the body.'

'Bloody hell,' said West. 'He's like Buchanan. He's had a stroke.'

* * *

Mick, enjoying the spectacle from his ringside seat on the 'police only' side of the cordon, smiled at Munro like a kid at the circus as he squatted down beside him.

'You're the chief, right?' he said. 'Probably an Inspector. I can tell.'

'No, no,' said Munro, 'well, yes I am but I'm not on this case, we're just…'

'You have *an interest*, isn't that what they say?'

'Aye,' said Munro, allowing himself a laugh, 'that is what they say, Mick, you're quite right.'

'So, what do you reckon? Bad junk or just bad luck?'

'It's too early to say but if somebody's flogging a bad batch of whatever we could have bodies piling up all over the place.'

'Oh, it's a good job it's happened now, then,' said Mick, 'that'd make an awful stink in the summer.'

'It would that,' said Munro with a grin. 'So how about you? Are you okay? You're not in shock or anything?'

'No, no. Seen one dead junkie, you've seen them all. And I've seen a few. How about you? Are you okay?'

'Me?'

'Aye. Is it not stressful, doing a job like yours?'

'It has its moments,' said Munro. 'Tell me, the chap behind the screens, did you know him well?

'Hardly knew him at all,' said Mick. 'He's English, did you know that?'

'Aye, we did. How did you meet?'

'I bumped into him last night, down by the car park. He looked a wee bit… lost.'

'Lost? Did he say where he was going?'

'No, no. Not lost as in *I need a map*,' said Mick, 'lost as in *direction unknown*, as in he didnae have a clue about anything.'

'I see. So, what happened?'

'We came up here. This is where I hang out. Not many folk come this way so I can sit and read, undisturbed.'

'You enjoy reading?' said Munro.

'Oh aye. Keeps the old brain ticking. If you dinnae keep that muscle active it's the care home for you.'

'Is that so? And what are reading just now?'

'Poetry. I've never read it before. First time.'

'And are you enjoying it?'

'Och, it's brilliant,' said Mick. 'Thing is, it's got a reputation, right? Like it's only for toffs but the folk that think that are the folk who dinnae get it. But I get it. I get it all. Ted Hughes. Have you heard of him?'

'I have indeed,' said Munro, 'although I'm more a fan of Seamus Heaney myself.'

'Heaney? I'll look out for him next time I'm down the library. Unless one falls off the shelf in Waterstones.'

'I'll pretend I didnae hear that,' said Munro, smiling. 'So back to our friend, his name was Toby by the way, what happened when you got here?'

'Not much,' said Mick. 'We sat and talked. Or rather he talked. Actually no, he ranted like he had some dirty great chip on his shoulder. Kept on and on about how minted he was but he couldnae get his hands on the cash. Och, he seemed harmless enough so I let him haver until he ran out of breath.'

'And then?'

'He wanted some gear but I only had enough for myself. Don't get me wrong, I'm a generous person me, but sometimes you have to put yourself first. Am I right?'

'Indeed,' said Munro.

'So I sent him to the Quattro.'

'The Quattro?'

'Aye, the Audi Quattro,' said Mick. 'Clapped out thing. Comes by the car park most nights. He's the fella with the gear.'

'So that's where Toby bought whatever it was he took?'

'Right enough,' said Mick.

'Did you happen to know what he took?' said Munro.

'No idea but he was okay first time round.'

'First time?'

'Aye,' said Mick, 'must've been about seven o'clock I reckon. Then he went for a second hit some time early this morning. Next thing I know he's having one on his back, twitching and screaming. I felt helpless, the lad was writhing in pain but what could I do? I mean, I'm not a medic.'

'So, what did you do?'

'Called the police of course.'

'I'm glad you did,' said Munro, rubbing his chin as he deliberated his next question. 'Listen Mick, would you mind if I asked you a wee favour?'

'If it's to do with money, sorry pal but I'm skint.'

'No, no,' said Munro, 'see here, if Toby was sold something dodgy then there's every chance someone else could die.'

'Aye, right enough,' said Mick.

'Could be you.'

'Could be.'

'And you're not bothered?' said Munro.

'I'm cacking myself.'

'Good. So, here's the thing. I really need to have a wee chat with this chap in the Quattro and but I'll need your help.'

'You mean you want me to point him out?' said Mick.

'Aye.'

'No, no. That's going a bit too far.'

'I guarantee he won't see you. You won't be any danger.'

'It's not that,' said Mick, 'if you take him off the streets where am I going to score?'

'Good point,' said Munro. 'I hadn't thought of that.'

'Six o'clock. The car park.'

Chapter 15

Although Dougal enjoyed nothing more than wandering the rambling Scottish countryside – especially if it involved trout or perch and a bucketful of bait – standing on a beach with nothing to do while a bunch of forensics picked over the cadaverous remains of a junkie like a wake of vultures in the Serengeti was not his idea of the great outdoors. Grinning deliriously as they returned to the office, he bounded to his desk and flipped open his laptop as Munro settled on a seat beside West.

'You know Charlie,' he said softly, 'you dinnae have to be here, you know. If you need some time to yourself, we can cope.'

'I've told you, Jimbo, I'm fine. But thanks anyway.'

'What you need is a cup of hot, sweet tea. You're in shock.'

'What I need,' said West, 'is some lunch. I'm bloody starving.'

'Well I must admit, a wee bite wouldnae go amiss,' said Munro. 'Dougal, can you tear yourself away from that thing for a moment.'

'Boss. What's up?'

'I'll give you a clue: low blood sugar, dizzy spells and an inability to concentrate.'

'Diabetes?'

'Last chance.'

'Two bacon toasties coming up,' said Dougal. 'Just give me a minute while I… Miss. Email. That swab I took from Dubrowski? We've a positive match to the blood samples taken from Buchanan's mouth.'

West looked up and smiled broadly as the colour returned to her cheeks.

'I think I need to go and charge someone on suspicion of murder, don't you?' she said. 'Brown sauce on mine, please, Dougal. And get me two.'

'Charlie, as you're away downstairs will you see Mrs Carducci gets to the interview room please,' said Munro. 'I'll be along shortly.'

'No probs. Shall I meet you there?'

'No, no. You come straight back and have your lunch. I'll see to it.'

* * *

Munro waited until West was out of earshot before continuing.

'Dougal,' he said. 'A wee word before you go.'

'Boss?'

'I need an unmarked car and two officers out front at 5.45. Can you do that?'

'Nae bother, but why?'

'I'll tell you later. Now, there's something else. I want you to keep an eye on Charlie.'

'DS West? I dinnae follow, Boss. Has she done something wrong?'

'No, no, Dougal. She's had a bit of a shock, that's all.'

'Okay. What do you mean "a bit of a shock"?'

'The gentleman on the beach,' said Munro, hesitating as he lowered his voice. 'That Lyndhurst chappie. He was… he was a close friend of Charlie's.'

'Are you joking me?' said Dougal. 'I am surprised, I mean how on earth does someone like DS West get to know a low-life like that?'

'They were in a relationship,' said Munro. 'A long time ago.'

'Oh Christ, I never knew. Hold on, he's not the fella she was telling me about a few days back? The fella who…'

'The same,' said Munro, 'but Dougal, not a word mind. If she wants to tell you about it, let her do it in her own time. Got that?'

'Aye, of course. Mum's the word.'

'Good lad. So, I want the pair of you to pick up Heather Buchanan and run her up to the morgue so she can take a peek at Angus and when you get back, sort out a warrant for the address on Dalblair Road. Now, on you go.'

* * *

PC Anderson stood to one side and waited patiently outside the cell as West – angry, agitated and confused – stood in the doorway with her arms folded and legs astride glowering at Dubrowski.

'You are staring, Sergeant,' he said with a smirk, 'in my country is okay, but here…'

'Why did you kill him?' said West.

'Kill who? I am not killing anybodies.'

'Cut the crap,' said West, raising her voice, 'you've got bite marks on your fingers…'

'It was puppy dog from long time ago.'

'…and your DNA matches a blood sample taken from Buchanan's mouth.'

'Ah. So this is what we are calling overwhelming evidence?' said Dubrowski, grinning. 'Okay, It's true. I kill him.'

'Why?'

'For the monies of course.'

'I don't buy it.'

'It's true.'

'You're telling me you killed an old man for a couple of grand?'

'A couple of grand to you,' said Dubrowski, 'but a million dollars to me.'

'So how did you know he had the money with him? How did you know it was in the bag?'

'Because I packed it for him.'

* * *

Anita Carducci, her face still buried in her faux fur collar, sat with her legs crossed and her handbag nestling in her lap like a C-list celebrity who'd blagged her way to the front row of a catwalk show during fashion week in Milan. She stared aloofly at the ceiling as Munro, unimpressed by her insouciance, tossed an envelope on the desk, flung his jacket over the back of the chair and sat down.

'Would you like something to drink, Mrs Carducci?' he said, leaning back and folding his arms. 'A glass of water, perhaps?'

Anita, her focus fixed firmly on the light fitting, declined to answer.

'Do you understand why you're here?'

'Not really, no.'

'Okay,' said Munro, 'this is how it works. I'm going to ask you some questions and you're going to answer them. It's really very easy, you know.'

'And if I refuse?'

'Och, you're not obliged to say anything at all, Mrs Carducci. I'm sure you're familiar with the phrase "no comment", feel free to use it at will. Now, before we start you really should have a lawyer present.'

'A lawyer?' said Anita.

'Aye, you're entitled to one and in fact I'd recommend it. If you dinnae have your own I can appoint the duty solicitor if you like.'

'No, no,' said Anita. 'I've nothing to hide, let's get on with it.'

'Okay good. Let's start with your trip. So, first question for ten points, were you intending to travel alone or was somebody meeting you at the port?'

'I was travelling alone.'

'And would this have been your first visit to Norway?'

'No,' said Anita, sighing indifferently. 'I've been before.'

'And where did you go exactly?' said Munro. 'Oslo or Bergen, perhaps?'

'No. Some dump in the suburbs. Loddefjord if you must know.'

'Sounds like you hated it.'

'I did.'

'Even with Angus Buchanan for company?'

Anita, at risk of losing her composure, glanced furtively at Munro before returning her gaze to the ceiling.

'It was business,' she said, clearing her throat. 'Just a wee bit of business.'

'Of course it was. Something to do with the restaurant, I imagine?'

'Aye, that's right,' said Anita cagily. 'The restaurant.'

'Excellent,' said Munro. 'Let's move on to round two. Tell me about the bags.'

'The bags?'

'Aye, the bags dropped off at your salon by Kestrel Cars,' said Munro. 'The bags your receptionist tells me you collect shortly after they're delivered.'

'They're nothing to do with me. I just take them in. For a friend.'

'I see. And this friend's not Angus Buchanan by any chance?'

'No comment,' said Anita, sarcastically.

'And what do you do with the bags once you've collected them from the salon?'

'I pass them on, okay? I just pass them on.'

'Who to?'

'No comment.'

'Have you any idea what's in them?'

'No. They're sealed with cable ties.'

'That's very trusting of you,' said Munro.

'I'm a very trusting person, Inspector. I look for the good in people.'

'That's interesting because I'm the opposite. I look for the bad. And I often find it. Let's talk about the other deliveries to your salon. The post addressed to Remus Trading.'

'Look, I was doing him a favour…'

'Mr Buchanan?'

'…aye, Mr Buchanan.'

'And does your husband know that Mr Buchanan is still operating the account?'

'No,' said Anita, her nerves fraying. 'Look, I was only trying to help. Angus asked if he could use the address and said all I had to do was…'

'What about the transfers?' said Munro, upping the tempo.

'What transfers?'

'The bank transfers from the Remus account to a bank account in Norway.'

'Norway?' said Anita, exasperated. 'Och, how would I know about that?'

'Just a hunch, Mrs Carducci. You see, the account in Norway is held at a branch of the DNB which happens to be in Loddefjord.'

'Sorry, Inspector, nothing you're saying is making any sense, you'll have to…'

Anita's words came to an abrupt halt as Munro pulled an iPad from the envelope sitting on the desk.

'Do you know what fascinates me most about these things, Mrs Carducci?' he said. 'It's not the amount of unbelievable technology sandwiched between a couple of sheets of glass and aluminium. No. You see what I find amazing about them is how careless their owners are when it comes to security. Take this one for example, it's not been switched off so all I had to do was open the browser to see what they'd been up to.'

Munro held up the iPad and showed it to Anita. Her face blanched at the sight of a web page bearing the Clydesdale Bank logo and a list of all the transfers from the Remus account to one held by a Mr Lars Gundersen.'

'This is your iPad, Mrs Carducci. Perhaps you'd care to explain?'

'I… it must have been Remo…' she said, stumbling over her words. 'He must've…'

'You just told me he thought the Remus account had been closed.'

'I must be mistaken.'

'I'm inclined to agree,' said Munro. I think you've mistaken me for a fool. See here, the transaction at the top of the list? It was made last night at one minute to midnight while Remo was down the pub getting blootered. He told me himself he didnae get home until after one.'

Anita, squirming in her seat, looked blankly at Munro and conceded defeat.

'Okay,' she said, her voice quavering. 'I did it. I transferred the money for him but I havenae done anything wrong. I was just doing the man a favour.'

'That's very charitable of you,' said Munro, 'but did you not think it odd he asked you to do it? I mean, why not do it himself?'

'I… it never crossed my mind.'

'Were you not intrigued by the sums involved?' said Munro. 'Did you not wonder where on earth Mr Buchanan could have got his hands on such large amounts of cash? Were you not just a wee bit curious what he was up to?'

Anita, looking as though she'd been stabbed in the back with a blunt pair of scissors, stared helplessly at Munro.

'No,' she said, bewildered by it all. 'I never even gave it a second thought.'

Munro, convinced she was a victim of nothing more than her own rose-tinted foolishness, smiled sympathetically.

'Tell me, Mrs Carducci,' he said. 'Why exactly were you going to Loddefjord?'

'To meet Angus. He's already there. He said one of his bags had gone missing and he needed help tracking it down.'

'One of his bags?'

'Aye, the blessed bags that came to the salon.'

'So they came here from Norway?'

'Och I've no idea, okay? Maybe. I don't know.'

'And it was Angus bringing them over?' said Munro.

'I don't know,' said Anita flatly. 'Look, all I know is Angus said a bag's gone missing and he reckons Tomek's taken it.'

Munro flinched.

'Tomek?' he said. 'Tomek Dubrowski?'

'That's right.'

'Mrs Carducci, why would Mr Buchanan be going to Norway to see Tomek Dubrowski when he lives right here?'

'Because Tomek has a flat there. In Loddefjord.'

Munro stood, tucked the chair beneath the table and took a deep breath as he clasped his hands behind his back.

'Okay,' he said. 'Here's where we are. Pending further questioning, at some point during the next twelve hours you will be…'

'Twelve hours?' said Anita. 'Twelve hours in that pokey cell?'

'I'm afraid we can't upgrade you to the presidential suite until you're formally charged, Mrs Carducci.'

'Charged?'

'Aye. As I was saying, pending further questioning, at some point during the next twelve hours you will be formally charged.'

'What with?'

'Well, we'll stick with being an accessory after the fact for now,' said Munro. 'We can always add to it later.'

'What do you mean? Add to it?'

'Well, depending on the outcome of our investigations, we may embellish it with handling stolen goods perhaps. Or money laundering. Or…'

'Are you joking me?' said Anita.

'I'm not a comedian, Mrs Carducci.'

'But I've told you, I've not done anything wrong.'

'Then you've nothing to worry about, have you?'

'Wait until I get my hands on him,' said Anita, grinding her teeth as her Italian temperament boiled over. 'I'll skelp the wee bastard.'

Munro looked on as she pulled a handkerchief from her bag and wiped the sweat from her palms, shuddering as his penetrating gaze caught her unawares.

'Final question,' he said, his voice menacingly low. 'How long have you and Mr Buchanan been having an affair?'

Anita, stunned in to silence, shied away in embarrassment.

'Mrs Carducci. How long have you and Mr Buchanan been having an affair?'

'Years,' said Anita. 'Longer than I can remember.'

'Your husband. And Mrs Heather Buchanan. I assume they know nothing about it?'

'No. They've no idea,' said Anita, switching her attention to the floor. 'It wasnae meant to… I didnae think it would last. It was just a drunken wee fumble at first but… well, here we are.'

'You must be fond of him.'

'Aye. I am Inspector. He's not like Remo. Don't get me wrong, I still love my husband, I always will, but Angus is different. He's not out to impress folk. He doesn't care for fancy cars or designer clothes. He's grounded, you know? Solid.'

'I see.'

'Heather's a lucky woman, Inspector,' said Anita. 'Very lucky indeed.'

'Not any more, she's not,' said Munro. 'I'm sorry to have to tell you this Mrs Carducci but Angus Buchanan is dead.'

Chapter 16

There were some things in life Munro could not stomach. Literally. Cold baked beans. Cold Scotch pies. And cold bacon sandwiches. The crusty specimen lying on the desk was, despite his hunger, simply not enticing enough to tempt him into sating his appetite. Berating himself for wasting food, he threw it in the bin and checked his watch.

'Dougal,' he said, answering the phone, 'is everything okay?'

'Aye, just to let you know we're running Mrs Buchanan home right now.'

'How is she?'

'She's fine. DS West wants to know if we should head back to the office after or…'

'No, no,' said Munro. 'Tell her to go home and Dougal, stay with her, would you?'

'Right you are. We'll not be long, will we see you there?'

'In a while. There's something I have to do first.'

* * *

Munro briefed the officers in the unmarked Astra, glanced casually around the car park and ambled towards the promenade, drawn towards a solitary figure sitting on the ground with a polystyrene cup in his hand.

'How are you, Mick?' he said, as he dropped a handful of coins wrapped in a twenty pound note into the cup.

'Aye, all good Inspector,' said Mick without looking up, 'he'll be along shortly.'

'Okay listen,' said Munro staring out to sea, 'when he arrives I need to have him stop a wee while, just long enough for us to reach him. Twenty seconds, that's all we need.'

'Are you saying you want me to approach him?'

'Aye, as you would normally. You've nothing to fear.'

'Are you sure?' said Mick.

'Positive. I'll be right behind him and there's a couple of other officers already in position. We'll not move until we see you doing a deal. Then all you have to do is act surprised and leg it, okay?'

'Sounds a wee bit risky to me. I'm not that good at running.'

'Trust me, Mick. You'll be fine.'

* * *

With the light fading fast, Munro – his patience wearing thin – cursed under his breath as one by one the workers and day-trippers drove off leaving him without the necessary cover he needed to maintain an element of surprise when all of a sudden Mick, who appeared to have been hibernating beneath his over-sized parka for the last forty-five minutes, jumped up and marched purposefully towards the car park.

Munro started the engine and tailed the Quattro, hemming it in as it stopped alongside the pay-and-display ticket machine and smiling at the sight of the unmarked Astra executing a novice's interpretation of a three-point turn dead ahead of it.

Mick, never keen on courting trouble, hovered nervously by the passenger door waiting for the window to open when, in a fearless act of self-preservation, he opted to take his leave as a staggered Munro, yanking open the driver's door, was left reeling at the sight of a portly, bespectacled gent in his late fifties smiling placidly like a librarian accepting a book two days before the due date.

'It's not aspirin you're selling by any chance, is it?' he said, as one of the officers slipped into the passenger seat. 'Only I've an awful headache coming on.'

'I'm afraid not,' said the driver as he reached inside his jacket, 'but I do have something that'll take the pain away.'

'No, no, no,' said Munro, 'hands on the wheel where I can see them.'

'It's my inhaler. For the asthma,' said the balding driver. 'Not the best ailment to be afflicted with if you suffer from stress.'

'Dinnae move a muscle,' said Munro as he reached in and retrieved it from his coat. 'Judging by the look on your face I assume you know why we've stopped you?'

'Well it's not because I failed to purchase a ticket from that machine.'

'Where is it?'

'Under the passenger seat.'

The officer reached down between his legs, pulled out a brown paper bag reeking of fried chicken and whistled at the stash of individually wrapped packages rolling around inside. He turned to Munro and nodded.

'Okay,' said Munro, 'I've just the one question for you Mr…?'

'John.'

'Mr John?'

'Just John. I'm not a fan of formality.'

'And I'm not a fan of yours just now. *John*. Question: were you here last night?'

'I was.'

'And did you sell any of this junk to a well-spoken fellow with an English accent?'

'As a matter of fact, I did.'

'Good. And how familiar are you with legal terms and definitions?'

'Oh I'm not quite sure, like what, for example?'

'Involuntary manslaughter,' said Munro. 'Take him away.'

* * *

West, stifling a yawn as she did her best to look interested, showed remarkable restraint in sipping a glass of red instead of knocking it back as Dougal, having hijacked her laptop, showed her the scenery surrounding the well-stocked Kilbirnie Loch brimming with pike, roach and trout, his enthusiasm propelled by the shot of a young girl in waders carrying a keep net on the home page. The sound of the front door slamming provided her with a much-needed escape route.

'What kept you?' she said, draining her glass as Munro hung his coat in the hallway, 'we've been getting worried.'

'All in good time,' said Munro as he sauntered into the kitchen, 'all in good time.'

'Dougal tried calling but you didn't pick up.'

'Good grief, can a man not have any privacy?'

'Ah-ha!' said West, grinning. 'I don't suppose this has anything to do with a certain Miss McClure, does it?'

'It most certainly does not,' said Munro. 'Now, if it's not too much trouble, two fingers please Charlie, I'm in dire need of some refreshment. Dougal, you look like you've bitten a lemon, what's wrong?'

'Nothing serious, Boss,' said Dougal as he closed the laptop, 'just backache.'

'Backache?'

'Aye, there's not much room in the back of that Figaro, no offence, Miss, but it's only built for two. I had to sit sideways in the back with my knees on my chest.'

'You're lucky it was just your knees laddie,' said Munro, gasping with pleasure as the whisky hit the back of his throat. 'And how was Heather Buchanan?'

'Yeah, she was fine,' said West. 'A bit upset at seeing her husband laid out like a turkey on a basting tray but she seemed to cope with it.'

'And she made the ID?'

'Yup.'

'And how about Dubrowski?' said Munro.

'Charged. But…'

'But what?'

'I don't know. I mean he admitted killing him just like that,' said West as she snapped her fingers, 'but he claims he did it for the money.'

'Must've been desperate,' said Dougal.

'No, no,' said Munro, 'something's not right here. If it was just the money he wanted why did he not just take it? There was no need to kill the poor chap.'

'Exactly,' said West. 'And that's what's bugging me. Anyway, I'm too tired to think about it now. How'd you get on? With Anita Carducci?'

'Guilty as hell but to be honest, she knows nothing about Buchanan's shenanigans.'

'To be fair, nor do we.'

'Right enough,' said Munro, 'but the fact that she agreed to have those mysterious bags and the post delivered to her salon without even raising an eyebrow makes her an accessory after the fact nonetheless. She's also admitted making the transfers between the Remus account and Gundersen's.'

'Well she had to really, didn't she?' said West. 'I mean the evidence was all on her iPad but what gets me is how she got involved in the first place.'

'Easy. Buchanan talked her into it.'

'So he was keeping his nose clean by hiding behind her?'

'Aye, and that's not all he was doing her behind her. The two of them have been at it for years.'

'No way!'

'All the way by the sounds of it.'

'The saucy cow.'

'So, Buchanan's the one responsible for bringing the stuff over from Norway?' said Dougal.

'Aye. Whatever that stuff may be. He's the one who organised it.'

'So we still don't know what was in the bags?'

'Not for certain but something tells me it's methamphetamine. Refill please, Charlie. What are you smiling at, lassie?'

'Dougal's got some news for you, haven't you, Dougal?'

'I have indeed. Dubrowski's flat, Boss; it's not his, he rents it.'

'Does it make a difference?'

'Aye, it does,' said Dougal. 'Especially when it's owned by Remo Carducci.'

'Mother of God? Carducci? Charlie, pass me the bottle.'

Munro poured himself another dram and walked to window.

'Buchanan I could understand,' he said ponderously as he stared at his own reflection, 'but Remo Carducci? What the blazes has he to do with anything?'

'Maybe nothing,' said West. 'Maybe Buchanan was using the flat without his knowledge. Either that or someone's hiding something.'

'You're not wrong there, lassie. So tell me, what should we do next?'

'Put the dinner on.'

'Not the answer I was looking for but it's worth a bonus point. Dougal?'

'Pay Carducci a visit?'

'No, no, no,' said Munro impatiently. 'I mean yes but more importantly…?'

West looked at Dougal and shrugged her shoulders.

'Good grief,' said Munro. 'Dougal, get on to your pals with the Loddefjord police and ask them to take a look inside that apartment. I'll be surprised if they dinnae find something of interest.'

'Right you are, Boss,' said Dougal, 'I'll email them now. Anything else?'

'Aye. A glass of red. A very large glass of red.'

'So come on then,' said West, handing him the wine, 'you've been awfully quiet about this evening's events, what have you been up to?'

'I've had a most rewarding evening at the beach with our friend Mick.'

'Mick?' said Dougal. 'You mean Mick the junkie from this morning?'

'I do indeed. And a very beguiling chap he is, too. Did you know he's into poetry?'

'Poetry?' said West.

'Aye, he's an educated chap. He's reading Ted Hughes just now. I recommended Seamus Heaney and I'm of a mind to fetch him a copy from the bookshop tomorrow.'

'So that's it?' said West. 'You spent the best part of the evening down on the beach talking poetry with a drug addict?'

'Not the entire evening, no. We had some other business to attend to.'

'God you're stretching this out,' said West, 'get on with it.'

'We've arrested the gentleman who murdered Toby.'

'What?' said West, flabbergasted.

'Well, when I say murdered I mean, indirectly,' said Munro. 'He's the fellow who sold Toby the gear. Had quite a stash with him too.'

'I don't know what to say.'

'Nothing is best.'

'Thanks,' said West as she eased herself onto a chair. 'I mean it. Thanks a lot.'

'Not necessary.'

'All the same, these dealers, the scabby little low-life runts in their pimped-up cars with wads of cash, they need to be...'

'Actually,' said Munro, 'he wasn't like that at all. To the contrary, he was quite a mature chap, fifty plus at least; in a clapped-out Quattro.'

'Really?'

'Aye. Took me by surprise too. Funny thing is, he actually seemed quite relieved to have been caught. I dinnae think the fellow was cut out for that particular line of work. Goes by the name of Kincaid.'

'Well, well done you,' said West, 'now let's eat. Dougal, you staying for dinner?'

'Och, I cannae stay, Miss,' said Dougal, 'it's getting late and I should be going.'

'Oh come on, there's plenty to go round. Lamb chops, mash and gravy.'

'You cannae argue with that, laddie,' said Munro, 'and you could do with beefing up.'

'Aye okay, go on then. Thanks.'

'Right,' said West, 'Dougal, plates over there. Jimbo, more wine please. Meanwhile, I shall... hold on just a minute, what the hell did you just say?'

'Me?' said Munro, looking surprised. 'I've not said anything.'

'Yes you did, the name. The name of the dealer you nabbed.'

'Him? Kincaid. John Kincaid. Why?'

'He's only their bloody accountant. Buchanan and Carducci. He's their sodding accountant.'

Chapter 17

There was a time when friends and neighbours would have queued up to eulogise about the mild-mannered John Kincaid who – with a talented daughter working overseas and an attractive wife whose career was on the up – once epitomised the archetypal family man until, that is, a chance meeting between a sales executive and Mrs Kincaid in a hotel in Bruges sparked the divorce which left his friends falling by the wayside and him wallowing in a one bedroom flat with nothing for company but a television set and severe depression. However, despite his losses and an overwhelming regret for having ever become embroiled in his somewhat illegal extra-curricular activities, he was intent on maintaining his dignity and sat with his tie firmly knotted, his hair combed and his hands resting on his ample belly.

'Mr Kincaid,' said West as she entered the interview room with Munro in tow, 'how nice to see you again.'

'Oh it's you, Sergeant, the feeling's mutual I'm sure. It's always nice to see a familiar face when one finds oneself in unfamiliar circumstances.'

'If you say so. This is Detective Inspector Munro.'

'I recognise you too, Inspector,' said Kincaid with a subtle nod. 'Are you not the gentleman who stopped me in the car park last night?'

'I am indeed,' said Munro, taking a seat. 'So, down to business. Do you know how this works, Mr Kincaid?'

'I've seen a bit on the telly but I'm not quite sure how accurate that is.'

'Okay, I'll keep it brief. Just tick the appropriate box: coffee, tea, lawyer?'

'I'm fine just now.'

'As you wish. Now, where shall we start?'

'I find the beginning is often the best place to start,' said Kincaid politely. 'Will I go first?'

Munro glanced at West and smiled, amused by Kincaid's ardent and frankly unexpected approach to the questioning.

'Be my guest,' he said. 'In your own time.'

'Right you are. Well, let's see. I've been an accountant for thirty-five years, roughly speaking, and that's an awful long time to be doing something that's neither stimulating nor financially rewarding.'

'Forgive me,' said Munro, 'but I was under the impression folk in your line of work earned what I'd refer to as a "king's ransom"?'

'I wish it were so, Inspector,' said Kincaid, his well-enunciated voice suggesting a background and an education somewhere near the top of the social ladder, 'unfortunately a couple of hundred pounds for preparing a company's returns isn't what I'd call satisfactory recompense for the work involved.'

'Well I stand corrected. So you were looking for other ways of supplementing your income, is that it?'

'Not intentionally, no. I certainly wasn't destitute but an opportunity presented itself which meant I could afford to provide a little more for my daughter and my wife. Ever since the divorce…'

'Sorry,' said West, interrupting, 'I don't mean to be rude but, divorce?'

'Aye. Last year,' said Kincaid. 'Fourteen months to be precise. It was quite the surprise I can tell you.'

'How so?'

'My wife. She met somebody else and announced she was leaving.'

'I don't follow,' said West, 'if she chose to leave you then why are you…'

'It's just my way, Sergeant,' said Kincaid. 'I've no idea if the fellow she's taken up with is capable of providing for her or my daughter and I do tend to worry so. That's why I gave her the house and the motor car.'

'You're too generous.'

'Perhaps, but it's my daughter that concerns me. She doesn't have much, working for a pittance thousands of miles away with orphaned orangutans or other such beasts. She's basically a volunteer so I send her something every month.'

'And where are you staying just now?' said Munro.

'I rent a flat in town. It's small but it's comfortable.'

'So money's a wee bit tight?'

'It can be a struggle, yes, so when I was propositioned…'

'To start dealing drugs?'

'I prefer to think of it as "the sale and distribution of reality-suspending supplements" but you're quite right of course, it's drug dealing by any other name and it was an opportunity too good to miss.'

'Okay, so let's get down to the nitty-gritty,' said Munro, 'who was it exactly that propositioned you? Was it one of those wee hard men who hang around the housing schemes or down by the river?'

'No, no. Actually it was an old client of mine. A Mr Carducci.'

'Carducci? Are you joking me?' said Munro, almost toppling from his seat as he scrambled to his feet. 'By jiminy, what the devil is that man playing at?'

'I'm not sure I follow, Inspector?'

'No, no, you're alright, Mr Kincaid. I'm just thinking aloud, that's all.'

'I see.'

'So when was this?' said West, 'I mean how long have you…?'

'Since the divorce really. The timing couldn't have been better. I'd just parted with a sizeable sum for the deposit on the flat, you see.'

Munro stood with his arms folded and his back to the wall wearing the kind of pained expression often associated with the thought of root canal surgery.

'Tell me, Mr Kincaid,' he said, 'who kept you supplied with the drugs? Was it Carducci himself or did you collect them from somewhere? A lock-up perhaps?'

'No, no. They were delivered to my office,' said Kincaid, 'sometimes a large padded envelope, sometimes a small holdall, that kind of thing.'

'Was that not a wee bit risky?'

'No. The other folk in the office simply assumed they were documents pertaining to work. Either that or I was away for the night.'

'And who delivered them to you?' said West. 'A courier? Not Kestrel Cars by any chance, was it?'

'No. Actually it was a rather attractive lady.'

'Really?' said West. 'You must have got to know her, what did you talk about?'

'We never spoke,' said Kincaid, 'she just smiled as she handed over the goods.'

'Do you have a name?'

'I'm afraid not but if it helps she was slightly younger than myself, I'd say. Dark hair and what I suppose you'd describe as Latin features. She may have been Spanish I think.'

'Anita Carducci,' said Munro.

'Anita Carducci?' said Kincaid. 'Would that be Mr Carducci's wife?'

'Aye, it would.'

'Well, well. I never realised it was a family business.'

'Nor did I,' said Munro, sighing as he returned to his seat. 'Nor did I.'

Kincaid, his lips pursed, looked at him and shook his head sympathetically.

'I must say, I don't envy you your job, Inspector,' he said, 'it seems awful complicated compared to mine.'

'You can say that again. Let's get back to your new career. So, you're away selling drugs to folk who cannae afford them and everything's going fine until the English gentleman expires on your patch and we arrive, is that it?'

'Pretty much, aye. That's about the size of it.'

West, intrigued by Kincaid's candour, leaned back in her seat, nibbled the top of her biro and regarded him curiously.

'What about the cash, Mr Kincaid?' she said. 'The cash you made from the punters, what did you do with that?'

Kincaid's eyes flashed furtively around the room before settling on his lap.

'I used to leave it in an envelope for her to collect each time she dropped off a new batch,' he said with head bowed. 'That's generally how it worked.'

'Used to?' said Munro with an inquiring tilt of the head. 'You *used to* leave it in an envelope. When did that stop? What changed?'

Kincaid's eyes dropped shamefully to the floor.

'It was another… opportunity,' he said. 'I can't think why I did it, I'm not impulsive by nature, you understand. It was a… mental aberration.'

'What was?' said West, growing impatient.

Kincaid took a deep breath.

'I was away for my lunch,' he said. 'When I returned to the office I noticed a small, black bag, the kind you'd carry a computer in, sitting by the side of my desk. I knew what it was immediately and one of my colleagues said the lady had dropped it off. I went outside and telephoned her. I asked of her, when was I to expect to the next delivery and as expected, she said she'd already been. Well, it was a rash thing to do, I realise that now, but I claimed not to have received it.'

'You were trying to pull a fast one?' said West, excitedly. 'You were trying to get one over on them?'

'I was,' said Kincaid. 'I thought if I could sell some of the goods myself and not have to settle for a paltry slice of the profits, I could relax about the rent and send some more to Catherine. That's my daughter.'

'So that's the missing bag,' said Munro.

'I beg your pardon?'

'Something Anita Carducci mentioned, that's all.'

'So what did she say?' said West. 'When you told her you didn't have the bag, I mean she must have been furious.'

'She was,' said Kincaid, 'but I thought to myself: what can she do? She couldn't very well return to the office and ask who'd stolen her drugs now, could she?'

'You crafty beggar. So what happened?'

'To use a term common to my chosen profession, Sergeant, they had to "write it off".'

'It's a dangerous game to play, Mr Kincaid,' said Munro, 'other folk would've had you bobbing in the Clyde by now.'

'I appreciate that, Inspector. I must admit, with hindsight, it probably wasn't one of my best ideas.'

'But you got away with it,' said West. 'Did you sell it all?'

'I did. But now that poor fellow's dead. I never to meant for anyone to die.'

'Well unfortunately they did,' said Munro, 'however, if it's any consolation, we've no other bodies to report so I doubt it was a bad batch. I'd say he probably suffered an adverse reaction to the stuff so chances are it would have happened sooner or later.'

'That's not much of a comfort, but thanks all the same.'

'Okay,' said West as she stood, 'I think that'll do for now, Mr Kincaid. Just to finish off, so far as you know, there's no-one else involved?'

'No, no. Not as far as I know.'

'And you've nothing to say in defence?' said Munro.

'I'm not here to protest my innocence, Inspector. I am, as they say, guilty as charged and I deserve everything I get.'

* * *

Munro stood to one side as Kincaid, smiling as though he'd successfully navigated his way through a particularly gruelling interview for the post of chief accountant with a multi-national conglomerate, was escorted back his cell.

'So come on, Charlie,' said Munro quietly, as he closed the door behind them, 'tell me what you think.'

West, leaning against the wall with both hands hanging from her belt loops, stared back, frowning as she rolled over the facts in her head.

'Okay,' she said, sagaciously. 'Wanna know what I think? I think Buchanan and Carducci were in this together.'

'I'm inclined to agree.'

'And I think Remo Carducci has played us perfectly. He's been stringing us along, acting like the innocent fool to keep us off his back.'

'Good,' said Munro, allowing himself a subtle smile, 'but they're not the only folk involved here. What else?'

'Okay. Anita Carducci and Angus Buchanan,' said West. 'They were having an affair, right?'

'Correct.'

'So I reckon, if it was Anita Carducci making the transfers from the bank and the money was going into an account held by Lars Gundersen…'

'Go on.'

'…and Angus Buchanan was carrying a passport in Gundersen's name, then the two of them were planning to do one. Run off together. Clear out the account and do one to Loddefjord. What are you grinning at?'

'You, lassie,' said Munro as he reached for the door. 'You've not only found your feet, you're standing on them too. I can see you'll not be needing me much longer. In fact, I think my work here is done.'

'Oh no, no,' said West, 'you don't get out of it that easily, we're not done yet.'

'We'll see. So, what's your next move?'

'We need another word with Carducci, but not at home. We need to bring him in.'

'And?'

'And what? That's it. Why are you shaking your head?'

'What about Buchanan?' said Munro.

'What about him? He's dead.'

'Precisely. But he didnae die of natural causes, did he?'

'Well, no,' said West, 'he was murdered.'

'By whom?'

'It's obvious, isn't it? Dubrowski. He topped him for the money.'

'Really?'

'Yeah, of course, that's what he… no. That's not it, is it? Too easy. Kill someone for a couple of grand in foreign currency?'

'Come on,' said Munro. 'I can hear your brain ticking from here, lassie. Get to it.'

'It was death by meth,' said West, biting her bottom lip, 'so… got it! Dubrowski didn't kill Buchanan off his own back. Someone told him to do it.'

'Nearly there.'

'It was Carducci. Remo Carducci!'

'At last. First prize goes to the lassie with the tortured brow. Shame it's not a car with plenty of legroom. Now all you need is a motive.'

'A motive?' said West, groaning with frustration. 'Oh, for crying out loud, dammit! I was on a roll and now I'm stuck.'

'You're not stuck, Charlie. Just think.'

'I can't, brain's gone dead. You know, don't you? Well, don't keep it to yourself.'

'Far be it for me to proffer an opinion,' said Munro, 'but if our friend Mr Buchanan was syphoning off the money with the help of Anita Carducci to finance their new future together then…'

'Then Remo must have known what they were doing!' said West, grinning as the penny dropped. 'He knew they were taking the money or… or he knew they were having it away together. Or both. And that's why he wanted rid of him.'

'You've redeemed yourself, lassie. Well done. So what will you do now?'

'Damn. We need to see Dubrowski before they take him away.'

* * *

Dubrowski, intimidated by the ominous silence, dropped the cocky expression he was so fond of wearing and regarded West with a look of concerned confusion as Munro, standing behind her, glared at him for what seemed like an eternity.

'Who told you to kill Angus Buchanan?' said West bluntly.

Dubrowski glanced at Munro and smirked.

'Nobody is telling me this,' he said as his arrogance resurfaced, 'as I say before, I am doing it for the monies.'

'Where did you get the rock from?'

'The rock?'

'The crystal meth you rammed down his throat.'

'I…'

'You see, Mr Dubrowski, if it was the money you were after, you could've just mugged him and legged it.'

'Yes, maybe, but then he is knowing it is me who…'

'So you killed him?' said West. 'So he couldn't identify you? Fair enough. Things is, I could understand it if you'd stabbed him. Or strangled him. Or broken his neck, even. But the meth?'

'It gives him heart attack,' said Dubrowski, 'it makes it look like…'

'Cut the crap. Last chance. Who gave you the meth?'

'I am having no comment.'

Munro, still glowering, took six slow, measured steps towards Dubrowski and stopped by his side.

'I know something you don't,' he said, his voice low and threatening, 'you see, the gentleman who gave you the rock, Mr Dubrowski, has *mislaid* an entire batch of meth. And this gentleman believes someone he knows may have stolen it. As you can imagine, he's not happy. Not happy at all.'

'What has this to do with me?'

'This gentleman has associates on the inside. In prison. The same prison where we've reserved a room for you. See here, Mr Dubrowski, if he thinks it was you who stole his meth then chances are, you'll not live long enough to see your next birthday. Do you get what I'm saying?'

'It was not me!' said Dubrowski, panicking. 'You must tell him, I did not steal drugs. I am a loyal person, I…'

'You're on your own, pal. Trust me. When he finds out it was you…'

'It was Clare!'

'What?' said West, 'Clare MacAllister?'

'Tak.'

'Your… girlfriend?'

'Tak. She tells me Mr Carducci has been good to me and now he is needing a favour. She is giving me the rock and telling me how to use it. She says if I do not do it then Mr Carducci will be coming for me.'

* * *

'Was that true' said West, as they made their way up to the office.

'Was what true, Charlie?'

'That bit about Carducci having mates on the inside.'

'I've no idea, lassie. Probably not.'

Chapter 18

Dougal – still salivating over the lamb chops and mashed potatoes – had come to realise that there was more to life than fish-paste sandwiches, bacon toasties or take-away curries and sat trawling the web for fool-proof recipes that a novice like himself could master without torching the kitchen when Munro and West breezed into office.

'Shepherd's pie,' he said. 'Did you know it's just mince and tatties?'

'You what?' said West.

'Shepherd's pie. It's a piece of cake.'

'I think you're confusing that with a gateau,' said Munro. 'What the devil are you blethering about, laddie?'

'I was looking for stuff to cook, easy stuff even I could do.'

'And what's brought about this irrepressible urge to make a mess in kitchen?'

'Last night. Cannae thank you enough, Miss. I never appreciated just how easy it is to whip up a decent meal if you're willing to make the effort.'

'It was my pleasure,' said West, 'but next time there will be a service charge.'

'I'd not complain about that. Anyway, I've some news for you two…'

'Just a moment, Dougal,' said Munro, raising his hand. 'Clare MacAllister. She's in collusion with Remo Carducci. If we're to take Dubrowski at his word, it was Clare who told him to kill Buchanan, at Carducci's request.'

'Really? So she's not just a humble manageress, then?'

'Apparently not. Have her brought in as soon as possible.'

'Right away, Boss. Now, I've a couple of things for you: first of all, Heather Buchanan – she's locked herself out.'

'Can she not get a locksmith?' said Munro.

'Maybe, if she knew where to find one.'

'Well, what about uniform? Surely this is more up their street?'

'I tried,' said Dougal, 'but she's not having it. She's in an awful state, Boss. Kept asking for you. She went to the Carducci residence to pick up a spare set of keys but no-one's answering.'

'Well maybe he's left for Italy already.'

'I hope not,' said West.

'Okay,' said Munro, 'tell her to stay put. We're going there now, we'll see her home.'

'Right you are. Second thing,' said Dougal, 'the Hordaland Police have been in touch, you'll not believe what…'

'James, Charlie, Dougal. I do hope I'm not interrupting,' said DCI Elliot as he blew through the door, 'I'll not keep you long.'

'No, you're alright, George,' said Munro, 'is something up?'

'Yes and no.'

'Is this to do with the case?' said West.

'Yes and no.'

'By jiminy,' said Munro, 'did you go to the same school as young Dougal here? What is it, man?'

'I just came to ask if you'd plans afoot to arrest anybody else, only we're full up.'

'Sorry?' said West.

'No room at the inn. Booked out. Your guests have taken all the cells.'

'Dinnae fret,' said Munro, 'one of them's about to check out.'

'Thank goodness for that. What about the others? Only the boys downstairs have a couple of fellas looking for a cancellation, they need somewhere to rest for a couple of hours before they take a tour of the courthouse.'

'We'll get Dougal to sort it,' said West, 'a couple of charge sheets and they should be on their way too.'

'Good, good. So you're making progress then?'

'Aye, the slow and steady kind,' said Munro.

'Excellent. Well, I'll leave you to it then,' said Elliot. 'Thanking you.'

'Sorry, Dougal, as you were saying,' said Munro, slightly bewildered.

'We've a report back from the Hordaland Police on the flat in Loddefjord. They're over it like a rash and they've sent some pictures too if you're interested.'

'Not just now, laddie, we have to pick up Remo Carducci and give his wife's salon the once over too, so let's just have the details, chop chop.'

'Right you are. First off, they doubt anyone's actually living there.'

'Meaning what?' said West. 'Is it run down? Empty? Abandoned?'

'No, no. It's clean and well furnished,' said Dougal, 'but there are no personal possessions. No clothes, no pictures on the wall, not even a bar of soap in the bathroom.'

'Not what you'd call a home, then?'

'Not unless you're a minimalist.'

'And that's it?'

'No, here's the best bit. Thanks to Andras…'

'Andras?' said Munro. 'Who the devil is Andras?'

'Andras is a Belgian Malinois,' said Dougal. 'She's a sniffer dog, Boss, and guess what? She found a stash of methamphetamine in the drawer under the cooker.'

'Are you joking me?'

'No. And it's not a small amount either. It was seven kilos.'

'Och, Dougal, that means nothing to me,' said Munro. 'For all I know these junkies could get through a kilo a night.'

'Okay, try it another way. The street value of this stuff is somewhere between fifteen and twenty grand a kilo.'

'Twenty grand a kilo?' said Munro, his eyes wide with astonishment, 'Jumping Jehoshaphat! How easy is it to make this junk, Dougal? Do you think we've an opportunity now that Buchanan's out of the way?'

'Might be a conflict of interest there, Boss,' said Dougal with a smirk. 'I'm afraid there's some bad news too.'

'Bad?' said West, 'What could possibly be bad?'

'The Hordaland Police; they're submitting a formal request to have Carducci extradited.'

'You what?' said West. 'How? Why?'

'Suspicion of drug trafficking, Miss. They want Tomek Dubrowski, too.'

'Well they're too late so far as Dubrowski's concerned,' said Munro. 'They can have him once he's served his sentence and as for Remo Carducci, don't you worry about him, laddie. It'll be days before that request gets to the Crown Office and even longer before they issue a warrant. We'll have him by then, trust me.'

'We should go,' said West. 'Heather Buchanan's waiting and I'm starving.'

'Nothing new there, then,' said Munro. 'Dougal, we've no time to look at the hair salon, you go. Give it a thorough once over, you're looking for anything to do with Remus Trading, okay?'

Chapter 19

With her coat buttoned to the neck, a shopping trolley by her side and her face filled with frustration, Heather Buchanan, looking to all intents and purposes as though she'd missed the last bus home, raised her eyes to the heavens and breathed a sigh of relief as Munro's antiquated Peugeot rolled to a halt behind the Carrera.

'Och, Inspector, thank goodness you're here,' she said as he'd barely stepped from the car, 'I feel such a fool. What must you think of me?'

'It's no big deal, Heather, honestly. I've done it myself.'

'I only noticed when I got back from the shops. I must have left them on the kitchen table when I gathered up my purse and my shopping list.'

'So you came all the way here?' said West. 'Bet you could do with a sit-down.'

'I'll not relax until I'm home, Sergeant. Remo and Anita keep a spare set, you see, so I came to get them but he's not answering the door.'

'Well he's probably away getting a few things for his trip,' said Munro. 'You know he's away to Italy for his father's birthday?'

'Aye, but that's not until tomorrow,' said Heather. 'Why's he not here?'

'It's okay, Mrs Buchanan,' said West, 'no need to worry. Like the Inspector says, he's probably just nipped out. Tell you what, why don't you wait in the car and we'll see if there's a way in round the back.'

'What if there isn't? What will I do then?'

'Heather, if we cannae get in here,' said Munro, 'we'll run you home and I'll see what we can do. I may have to break a window but it's nothing worth worrying about. Okay?'

'Aye, okay, Inspector. You know best.'

'Good. Now if we do get in, where does Mr Carducci keep your keys?'

'Kitchen drawer, the one by the sink. There's a wee tag with our name on it.'

* * *

Munro stood for a moment and cast an approving though somewhat envious eye over the back garden – a sprawling affair with a lush lawn surrounded by mature beds and well-stocked planters – and wondered if he had the wherewithal to emulate it at home as West rattled the door before calling excitedly at the sight of a side-opening window slightly ajar.

'Jimbo!' she said. 'Thank God for proper windows, we'd have had it if they'd replaced them with those pig-ugly PVC jobbies. We need a stick or something to lift the stay then we're in.'

'Right you are, lassie,' said Munro as he pulled a bamboo stake from the flower bed and handed it over. 'I never realised you were so adept at house-breaking.'

'It's not a misspent youth, if that's what you think,' said West, 'more a case of having to sneak back in without my parents noticing. Right, off you go.'

'Me? I'm not the India Rubber Man, Charlie. Besides, I think this is a job for someone marginally younger than myself.'

'But you're considerably taller than me, you don't have to climb over the sink, you could reach round to the door.'

'Have you no respect for your elders?' said Munro as he pulled off his jacket. 'This is tantamount to abuse. Drag that bench over and we'll give it go.'

Munro climbed on the bench and eased himself through the open window, inadvertently clearing the draining board of several items of crockery as he went and, from West's point of view, looking like a terrier stuck down a rabbit hole.

'Well done, Jimbo! she said, as she heard the latch lift on the door, 'I'm coming in.'

'Mind the broken glass,' said Munro as he climbed down, 'and look for a broom while you're there, lassie. We dinnae want a claim for compensation coming our way.'

* * *

'Right, here we are,' said Munro as he opened the front door, 'we'll see you in safe, make sure you're settled.'

'Och, there's really no need, Inspector,' said Heather as she hung her coat, 'you've done enough already.'

'It's no trouble,' said West, 'here: keys. Put them somewhere safe.'

'I will, dear. I'll make sure of that.'

'I think you deserve a cuppa now, don't you? You sit yourself down and we'll stick the kettle on.'

'But I'm keeping you from your work, there's really no need.'

'Do as the Sergeant says, Heather,' said Munro, smiling as he emptied the shopping trolley, 'you've had quite a day. Now, will I fetch you a biscuit or something? A slice of bread and butter, perhaps?'

'No, you're alright,' said Heather, staring into space. 'I'm not hungry just now.'

'Are you okay?' said West as she pulled up a chair, 'you seem a bit... is there someone we can call? Someone who can come over for a while?'

'No dear. Anita's away now…'

'She certainly is,' said Munro.

'…so that's it. There's no-one else. Only Tommy.'

'Tommy?'

'Aye, he's my brother.'

'Your brother?' said Munro. 'For heaven's sake Heather, why did you not mention him before? We could've called him days ago.'

'He's not one for family, Inspector. Or socialising, for that matter.'

'Aye, but even so, I mean after what you've been through, surely…'

'I did try calling him. Just the once, I admit, but there was no answer.'

'Will I send for him? It's no bother.'

Heather thought for a moment and smiled wistfully.

'Aye, okay,' she said. 'I think I'd like that.'

'Good,' said Munro. 'Where does he stay?'

'Nowhere fancy. He rents a room in Souter Place.'

'Souter Place?' said West. 'That sounds familiar. Who should we ask for?'

'Tommy. Tommy Dubrowski.'

Chapter 20

'We came over as weans,' said Heather. 'My father, Tommy and myself.'

'And your mother?' said West.

'There were *complications*. She died shortly after Tommy was born.'

'I see.'

'My father raised us as best he could but the poor man really had no interest in anything anymore, especially home, so as soon as we were old enough, he brought us here.'

'Sorry, Heather,' said Munro. 'I'm a wee bit confused here. You were born in Norway but your brother has a Polish surname and yours is typically Scottish.'

'It's actually very simple, Inspector,' said Heather. 'My mother was Norwegian and my father was Polish. They met as students in Warsaw. He was studying engineering and she was visiting. After they were married they moved to Norway to be near my mother's parents. I was named after her: Hedzia. It means heather, or so I'm told. To be honest I've never really checked.'

'That's such a great story,' said West, 'so you came here, what happened next?'

'Och, I was having a ball. I fitted right in, had the time of my life but it wasnae easy for Tommy, he…'

Heather's eyes glazed over as she reminisced.

'…Tommy's not like the rest of us, you see. He's better now but he's never been right in the head, if you know what I mean. He didnae settle in well at all. The other kids poked fun at him because he was a wee bit slow so my father took him back to Poland. To a special school.'

'And he left you here?' said West. 'On your own?'

'Och, I was almost grown, Sergeant. Sixteen years old. I stayed with a very nice family but only until I was eighteen. Then I got my own place and as luck would have it, I met Angus not long after.'

'And Tommy?' said Munro. 'What happened to Tommy in the meantime?'

'We lost touch, of course. I had no idea where he was then I received a phone call, from a hospital in Norway.'

'Norway?' said West.

'That's right, dear. Once Tommy had finished school, they moved back. My father thought the more familiar surroundings might help Tommy adjust. Prepare him for the adult world.'

'I see. And the hospital?'

'They'd tracked me down. My father, unbeknownst to me, had passed on so I was his only surviving next of kin. And thank goodness they found me, that's all I can say. Lord knows what might have become of him otherwise. Naturally, it was only right and proper that I sent for him. I asked Angus to see him right, get him a job and take him under his wing. And he did, God bless him. Looked after him like a brother, he did.'

'It's shame his generosity wasnae reciprocated,' said Munro.

'I'm not sure I follow, Inspector.'

'I'm afraid Tommy's landed himself in a wee bit of bother.'

'Dearie me, whatever has he done? Is it serious?'

'Oh aye. It's about as serious as it can get, Heather. It's very serious indeed.'

* * *

West jogged lethargically back to the car, slumped in her seat and sighed disappointedly as she handed Munro a stick of Peperami and a packet of plain crisps.

'It's all they had,' she said, looking glum. 'Pub stopped serving food ages ago.'

'You have it, lassie,' said Munro, grimacing at what looked like a dog chew as he glanced across at Carducci's house, 'your need is greater than mine.'

'Still no sign?'

'Nothing. Not even a light on.'

'Well, he can't be far,' said West. 'We'll wait a while. How do you think she took it? Heather, I mean.'

'Well, she's not one for showing her emotions, that's for sure. I think she's still in shock, Charlie. It's not easy for her – learning about her brother so soon after losing Angus.'

'You're right, it must be doing her head in, poor thing. I feel sorry for her, sitting there all alone. Shame there's no-one she can call.'

'Oh, I think there probably is,' said Munro, checking his watch, 'she just chooses not to. Where the devil is he?'

'Getting impatient?'

'I'm not sitting here all night, Charlie. Give the man a ring, find out where he is.'

West held her phone aloft and cancelled the call as it rang through to voicemail.

'That's it,' said Munro, unclipping his seat belt, 'I'll not wait for that confounded Casanova a second longer. Let's take a look inside.'

'You sure?' said West. 'What if he comes by and finds us…'

'Och, it's not as if we're breaking and entering, Charlie. You're forgetting, there's a door open round the back.'

* * *

Rules, postulated Munro, were restrictions imposed on the hoi-polloi by those who deemed themselves superior by birth, class or privilege, and were there to be bent or broken as often as possible apart from just two which, he opined, were key to maintaining a stress-free existence and an unruffled relationship: "Never go to bed on an argument" and "Never wake up to another man's wife". Or for that matter, a hangover or the washing-up from the night before. He cast a disparaging eye around the dining room, appalled at the sight of the table littered with filthy plates, a scattering of olives, a half-eaten baguette, several slices of mortadella and a wedge of provolone which appeared to have been attacked with a hacksaw.

'Now that's a slippery slope,' he said, tutting as he glimpsed the single wine glass and two empty bottles of Chianti Classico. 'A wee glass or a couple of drams, fair enough, but two bottles? To yourself? The man has a problem.'

'Either that or he's marinating his liver from the inside,' said West. 'He'll probably end up frying it with a barrel load of onions and some Grand Marnier.'

Munro took a step back and, standing stock still, scoured the scene, his eyes narrowing as he absorbed every minute detail.

'Tell me what you see, Charlie,' he said, quietly. 'Apart from the remnants of an alcohol-induced feeding frenzy, tell me what you can glean from this.'

West glanced at the table and smiled.

'That he's crap at loading a dishwasher,' she said.

'That he had company, lassie. He may have been drinking alone but at some point, he had company.'

'How so?'

'The chairs. Two chairs pulled away from the table. And two mugs.'

West leaned over the mugs and sniffed.

'Coffee,' she said, 'and there's a smidge of lipstick on this one. A sort of plum colour.'

'Female company, then, which may explain his absence. Perhaps he's taken her home.'

'Not so sure about that,' said West. 'His car's out front and frankly, I can't see the likes of Carducci hopping on a bus.'

Munro ambled from the dining room and opened the door to his left, sneezing as the lavender-scented air freshener from the downstairs toilet accosted his nostrils.

'Excuse me,' he said, wiping his nose as he peered down the hallway, arrested by the sight of a cabin case sitting by the front door. 'Looks as though he's ready to go.'

'There's a travel wallet on the top, Jimbo,' said West, 'check his ticket and passport, make sure he's not travelling under an assumed name, too.'

'Excellent, Charlie,' said Munro, smirking as he looked over the documents. 'Who'd have thought a stick of Peperami could have such a positive impact on one's cognitive performance.'

'I've got one stick left,' said West, 'it could have a positive impact somewhere else if you're not careful.'

'He's all legit by the looks of it. His flight's tomorrow morning.'

'Gonna have a bit of a shock when his wife's not there to meet him.'

'I've a funny feeling, Charlie, he's not expecting her to be.'

West paused by the entrance to the lounge, prodded Munro with her elbow and nodded in the direction of an armchair where the back of somebody's head was just visible over the top.

'So that's why he's not answering the door,' she said.

'I'm not surprised,' said Munro, as he walked around the chair, 'after two bottles of red the fella's probably that blootered he'd not wake up if the house fell down around him. Rise and shine, Mr Carducci. Time for a game of twenty questions.'

Barring those in the midst of a troublesome nightmare, Carducci's expression was not one commonly worn by those in a state of blissful slumber which was, Munro concluded, probably due to the nine-inch carving knife protruding from his scrawny neck and the reason why his stupefied face retained such a ghostly pallor.

'Dear, dear, dear,' he said, staring at Carducci's lifeless body, 'when they say alcohol can kill I'm not sure this is what they had in mind.'

'Bloody hell,' said West as she inspected the wound, 'that's the worst tracheotomy I've seen in a long time.'

'Right, Charlie, SOCO's and uniform, please,' said Munro as he snapped on a pair gloves. 'And call Dougal, tell him we need him here yesterday. Chop, chop.'

Munro spun slowly on his heels, took a fleeting glance around the room and, satisfied there was nothing to suggest a disturbance of any kind, turned his attention to Carducci. He stood before him, hands clasped behind his back, squinting as he scanned the body from the ground up. The feet were positioned heels together, the polished leather loafers immaculate. His fawn-coloured chinos, though neatly pressed were marred by a spattering of crimson stains no doubt a result of the blood coughed up as he struggled to catch a breath. His gnarled hands, beset with rigor, were still gripping the armrests and his otherwise pristine shirt, buttoned at the collar, was blighted by a tide of red running the length of his chest.

'Sorted,' said West as she returned to the room, 'they're on the way. So, come on then, any thoughts?'

'Well,' said Munro, standing straight and rubbing his chin, 'at first I thought he had incredible posture for one so dead, but it appears whoever did this has actually pinned his neck to the back of the chair.'

'Ouch. Must've taken some force, then.'

'Not necessarily, Charlie. It's a quality knife. If the assailant had the element of surprise on their side too, well, one swift thrust would've done the job admirably. Incidentally, it's the same knife he used to slice the mortadella, I can see traces of fat around the hilt.'

'Nice,' said West. 'Don't think we'll be eating Italian tonight. Anything else?'

'Headphones, Charlie. What does that tell you?'

'That he may not have heard his attacker come in?'

'Either that,' said Munro, 'or he inadvertently played a song by Black Sabbath which would explain the look on his face.'

'Have you no respect?' said West, stifling a laugh.

'See here, his breast pocket. Is it me or is it glowing?'

West reached in and pulled out a mobile phone.

'Five unread texts,' she said, 'and four voice messages.'

'Well, I know it's rude to read other folks' mail but I think in this case we'll make an exception, don't you?'

West opened the texts, turned to Munro and frowned.

'Clare MacAllister,' she said. 'They're all from Clare MacAllister, sent last night.'

'This should be interesting,' said Munro. 'Go on.'

7:32pm You're late, handsome. Dinner in thirty x
8:05pm Where are you, it's getting cold and so am I x
8:42pm Okay you're held up. Just get in touch
9:52pm You can't be bothered so nor can I. Screw you
10:17pm That's it pal and don't you dare come knocking my
door

'So,' said Munro, smiling. 'it seems Senor Carducci and our friend Buchanan have more in common than we thought.'

'Indeed,' said West, 'I wonder what Dubrowski would say if he found out his girlfriend was cheating on him with her boss?'

'Och, I dare say he'll get over it, considering present circumstances. Shall we?'

'Silly not to, really,' said West as she held up the phone.

"You have two new messages. First message sent yesterday at 11:22pm"

'Listen, me again. I'm sorry, okay, but if you ever stand me up again there'll be hell to pay. Call me when you get this'

"Second message sent today at 7:29am"

'That's it, I've had it with you, you bawbag. I'm not some floozie you can call up anytime you fancy a bit of the other. I'm coming over and you're getting what's coming to you and no, I dinnae care if your wife's there, you're not messing with me again. And by the way, the restaurant's closed. I'm not opening it ever again.'

"End of message. To repeat your message, press…"

'Nothing like a woman scorned,' said Munro. 'Looks as though we have a suspect.'

'Not half,' said West, 'we'll give her a grilling when we get back, shall we?'

* * *

The doorbell – as loud as an ice-cream van belting out an annoyingly tinny rendition of *O Sole Mio* – heralded the arrival of Dougal who, still wearing his helmet and clutching a padded envelope, resembled a cross between a courier and a human cannonball.

'Alright, Miss?' he said as West opened the door. 'What's all the fuss?'

'Ever seen those knife-throwing acts at the circus, Dougal?'

'Aye.'

'Well this,' said West, 'is the one that went wrong.'

176

'Is it messy?' said Dougal, as he followed her to the lounge. 'Only I've not long eaten and I'm not sure a burger and a milkshake is heavy enough to stay down.'

Munro, scrutinising Carducci's neck in an effort to ascertain whether he was struck from the front or behind, looked up and smiled as Dougal walked tentatively around the chair to face the body.

'Oh, it's not as bad as I thought,' he said, 'no more than a wee stab wound really.'

'I've seen worse,' said Munro. 'Tell me Dougal, do the Carducci's have a cat? A ginger Tom by any chance?'

'I've not see one, Boss. Why?'

'Somebody's shed some hair on his shoulder. Red hair. Get it bagged for forensics, please. I want to know who it belongs to as soon as possible.'

'Right you are.'

'And there's a couple of mugs on the dining table, one of which has lipstick on it, same again. Now, how were things at the salon? Did you find anything of interest?'

'I did,' said Dougal. 'The receptionist was very helpful, we had a good long chat.'

'About Anita Carducci?'

'No, no. Fish. She's actually into fish.'

'Dinnae get your hopes up, laddie,' said Munro. 'I've met her. She probably likes them deep-fried. About four times a week, I'd say. What else?'

'This was under the cash tray in the safe,' said a disheartened Dougal as he handed him the envelope. 'It's the passport belonging to the real Lars Gundersen, it's good for another four years. And there's a couple of old bank cards. Expired. Just about bangs the final nail in the coffin, if you ask me.'

'Good grief,' said Munro, as he opened the passport, 'this fellow looks just like Angus Buchanan.'

'Aye. Well, apart from the nose, and a bit younger maybe. But let's face it, if you were immigration glancing at that, you'd not know the difference.'

Chapter 21

Contrary to popular belief, growing up in Berkshire wasn't all Royal Ascot and Windsor Castle, hikes in the countryside and joining the pony club. As West soon discovered, there were areas of the county which were just as fraught with danger as any other urbanised landscape but, being of an amiable disposition and inquisitive by nature, she enjoyed mingling with anyone, be it the lager louts of Slough or the stockbrokers of Bray, all of whom were charming enough in their own inimitable way, unlike certain residents who carried themselves with an arrogant air of self-importance – no doubt a consequence of their own insecurities – and delighted in belittling anyone they thought below them. Had Clare MacAllister lived in Berkshire, she'd have settled right in.

'Listen hen,' she said, fiddling with her fake Ray-Bans, 'I came here voluntarily so you'd best get on, I've a million and one things to do and I'm behind already.'

'I'm sure you are,' said West, 'but if you'd like us to make your stay a little more formal, just say so.'

'Are you threatening me?'

'No, madam. I'm simply extending an invitation.'

'Oh, I get it. I feel sorry for you,' said MacAllister. 'No, really I do. It can't be easy taking care of your appearance in your line of work. All that running about the place with no time to look in a mirror. It's bound to make you grumpy.'

'Quite,' said West, 'but to be perfectly honest, I'd rather look like the back end of a bulldog than clean tables all day.'

'Did you hear that?' said MacAllister. 'Did you hear what she just said?'

'I heard nothing untoward,' said Munro, smiling just enough to raise one corner of his mouth. 'Would you like to make a complaint?'

'I've never been so insulted.'

'You should get out more,' said West. 'Now, as you're so busy I suggest we crack on.'

'Aye, we better had. Before I crack something else.'

'Good. Just to let you know that when we're done here, we'll need a swab from the inside of your cheek for DNA purposes.'

'You're not sticking anything in my mouth,' said MacAllister, 'you can't do it.'

'I'm afraid we can. Now, where were we? Oh, yes. Why did you tell Tomek Dubrowski to kill Angus Buchanan?'

MacAllister drew a sharp breath and scowled at West.

'I did no such thing,' she said.

'He says you did.'

'Poppycock.'

'Do you know how Mr Buchanan died?'

'No idea,' said MacAllister, sighing impatiently. 'Surprise me.'

'Overdose,' said West. 'Crystal meth. Which, incidentally, Mr Dubrowski also claims you gave him.'

'Utter rubbish.'

'Okay, let me put it another way. Why did Remo Carducci want Mr Buchanan dead?'

MacAllister winced, glanced towards the door and said nothing.

'Miss MacAllister,' said Munro, 'apologies if I appear a wee bit slow on the uptake here, it's probably my age but you dinnae seem to be at all surprised to hear of Mr Buchanan's demise.'

'Should I be?' said MacAllister, clearing her throat.

'Perhaps not, but how could you possibly know he was dead?'

'You just told me.'

'Did we? Did we indeed?'

West glared across the table, leaned back in her chair and folded her arms as the silence bore down on MacAllister like a ten-ton weight.

'Last time we spoke you said you rarely saw Mr Buchanan,' she said, 'but Mr Carducci popped into the restaurant all the time.'

'Did I?'

'Yeah. You said you and he got on quite well.'

'I must've been on happy pills.'

'How long have you and Mr Carducci been having an affair?' said West.

'Are you joking me?' said MacAllister, raising her voice. 'You have got to be kidding. Me and that good-for-nothing greaseball?'

'Greaseball?' said Munro. 'My, my, that's no way to speak of your boss. Oh, and I think you'll find the word you're looking for is *bawbag*.'

'What?'

West, smiling sarcastically, held up Carducci's phone and played back the voicemail.

'*Bawbag*,' she said. 'The Inspector was right after all. So?'

'Couple of years, if you must know,' said MacAllister, defiantly. 'He didnae care about me, I was just some piece of fluff as far as he was concerned. Not that it's anything to do with you.'

'If that's what he thought of you, why didn't you end it?' said West. 'I mean, what with your busy schedule and all, I'm surprised you had time to fit him in.'

'Listen hen, one more comment like that and I'll…'

'What time did you arrive at Mr Carducci's house this morning?' said Munro.

'This morning?'

'Aye. You said in your message that you were heading over there this morning.'

'I didnae go,' said MacAllister as Munro glared back at her. 'I was nursing a wee hangover so I didnae go.'

'Well,' said Munro, hedging his bets, 'I've some red hair that says you did.'

'Are you joking me?'

'Nice lipstick,' said West, 'it really suits you.'

'Are you being funny?'

'No, really. It does. What's it called?'

MacAllister paused before answering, befuddled by the bizarre nature of the question.

'Hellraiser,' she said. 'It's called "Hellraiser".'

'How appropriate.'

'What time did you leave Carducci's place this morning, Miss MacAllister?' said Munro.

'For Christ's sake, are you deaf? I told you, I didnae go. Look, if you dinnae believe me, ask him yourself.'

'Och, I've already tried,' said Munro, 'but he's not very talkative just now. He has a sore throat.'

'Aw, poor wee man. Caught a cold, has he?'

'He's a cold everything, Miss MacAllister. He's dead. Stabbed through the neck sometime between seven a.m. and ten a.m. this morning. So, unless you can prove irrefutably where you were at that time, my advice to you is to contact your lawyer.'

* * *

Having forsaken his stick of Peperami in the optimistic hope of dining on something a little more palatable, and fearing he might faint as a result of his self-induced fast, Munro set about demolishing his sirloin with the gusto of a ravenous waif in a pie-eating contest, leaving West agog at the speed with which it vanished from his plate. He dabbed his mouth with a napkin, took a large sip of wine and let out a satisfied sigh as he eyed the lemon cheesecake sitting on the counter.

'I'm glad to see you finally got the hang of the cooker, Charlie,' he said with a wink, 'that was first class. Thank you.'

'Just needed a refresher course, Jimbo. I used to be quite a good cook once but if you don't have the time or the inclination you tend to forget.'

'Aye, right enough,' said Munro, 'that's my excuse when it comes to paying the electricity bill.'

'Were your days always this full-on?' said West. 'I mean, when I was down south everyone buggered of at six, what you'd call a *mañana* attitude.'

'It all depends on how much you enjoy your work, lassie. How determined you are to close a case with the right result. So yes, in answer to your question, my days have always been quite eventful.'

'And tomorrow?'

'What of it?'

'Are we gonna charge MacAllister?'

'With what?'

'What do you think?'

'We've no evidence, Charlie,' said Munro, 'not unless forensics come back with something positive. All we have right now is circumstantial.'

'Yeah, but we could hold her on suspicion,' said West. 'Let's face it, the woman's as guilty as sin.'

'Aye, maybe.'

'You're not convinced, are you?'

Munro drained his glass, sat back and placed his hands palm down on the table.

'Remember what I said a while back, lassie? About your instinct being the best tool in your box?'

'Yeah, of course,' said West, 'but what about the facts?'

'I'll give you some facts, Charlie. Fact: we know Lars Gundersen used to work as a driver for Remus and we know Dubrowski took over the role when he went missing. Fact: we know Buchanan was using Gundersen's identity to slip in and out of the country unnoticed. Fact: we know Dubrowski killed Buchanan. Fact: we know Carducci and Buchanan were bringing in meth from Norway and fact: MacAllister *probably* killed Remo Carducci but we cannae prove it.'

'Okay, okay, I get it,' said West, sighing as she topped up their glasses. 'You left out the fact that Angus Buchanan and Anita Carducci were planning to hop it with the proceeds of their activities.'

'Indeed they were,' said Munro, 'And Remo Carducci knew it. That's why he sent Buchanan off for a big sleep. Listen Charlie, I'm not having a go at you, all I'm saying is we didnae have the evidence to get a conviction on MacAllister but you must do what you feel is right. If you think she's responsible for knifing Senor Carducci, then you must charge her. Now, will we have that cheesecake or are we just going to look at it?'

Chapter 22

Not normally one for shopping lists as the only person he'd ever had to cater for hitherto was himself, Dougal – grinning inanely – was seated before his computer excitedly scribbling down a list of possible picnic ingredients, none of which were sandwiches but most of which were either deep-fried or wrapped in pastry with the combined ability to raise one's cholesterol levels or clog an artery within hours of consumption.

'Morning, Dougal,' said Munro as he shook the morning drizzle from his coat. 'You've the kind of shameless smile on your face a dear friend of mine once had when he was bequeathed a small fortune. What's your excuse?'

'Fishing, Boss. I'm away to the loch on Sunday.'

'And does the prospect of sitting on a bank normally induce such a state of euphoria?'

'No. This time's a wee bit different. This time I'll not be going alone.'

'Is that so? And who, if I may be so bold, is going to keep you company?'

'Lizzie,' said Dougal, his cheeks flushing. 'She's the receptionist from the salon. She texted me last night and asked if she could come along.'

'Good for you, Dougal!' said West. 'You go for it but, if you don't mind me saying so, isn't she a bit... young for you? No offence. I just...'

'None taken,' said Dougal. 'Beggars can't be choosers. Besides, she's not that much younger. A few years. I think.'

'Well, all I can say is I hope you've a panic button on your telephone,' said Munro. 'You'd stand a better chance of survival in a tankful of piranhas. Have you had yourself some breakfast yet, laddie?'

'No, not yet. I've been a wee bit... busy.'

'Would you mind doing the honours? Kitchen was closed at the Hotel Charlie this morning, we're awaiting supplies.'

'Nae bother, you can look through this while I'm gone,' said Dougal as he placed a brown paper sack on the desk. 'A few of Carducci's things, it came from the lab last night, they're done with them now. Oh, and we've had a spot of good news, too.'

'And what's that?' said Munro.

'The hair and the lipstick, they're a perfect match for MacAllister.'

West turned to Munro, mouth agape and slammed the table.

'Yes!' she said, 'told you, Jimbo. What did I say? I was right, wasn't I?'

'Aye. Maybe, lassie. Maybe.'

* * *

Munro tipped the contents of the sack onto the desk as Dougal left for the cafe and sifted through the individually bagged items with his index finger as West looked on.

'Knife,' he said, 'wallet, keys, phone...'

'Phone?' said West, the smile disappearing from her face. 'But we've got his phone. Give me that.'

She fired up the old Nokia handset and rapped the table impatiently as she waited for the screen to come to life.

'Damn it!' she said as she scrolled through the inbox. 'Battery's almost gone. Not a single text sent or received.'

'Call list,' said Munro. 'Check the call list.'

'Tons. All the same number. All beginning with four-seven-five.'

'Norway,' said Munro. 'Four-seven. That's the code for Norway. I'm guessing the five's for Loddefjord.'

'Then it must be his flat,' said West, 'but why keep a separate phone to call his flat when we all know he owns the place anyway?'

'We know why, Charlie. The man's not as stupid as he made out. Traceability.'

'Of course. Sorry, being thick. I wonder where they found it?'

'Probably in his trouser pocket,' said Munro. 'We couldnae move the poor chap, could we? He was tacked to the chair like a post-it note on a dartboard.'

West opened the wallet, raising her eyebrows as she fanned through the notes.

'Blimey,' she said, 'must be a few thousand euros here, all in five hundreds.'

'Is that so? Now why would somebody going to a wee village for a family celebration need so much cash?'

'Ego, I imagine,' said West. 'Knowing how flash he was I wouldn't be surprised if he was going to give it all away as a measure of his success.'

'Aye, you're probably right, lassie,' said Munro. 'You're probably right.'

* * *

Dougal, looking surprisingly downbeat considering his joyful mood just a few minutes earlier, returned to the office and handed out the sandwiches.

'Here we go,' he said sheepishly as he scurried to his desk. 'They're all the same. Sausage on white bread.'

'What's up?' said West. 'Two minutes ago you were over the moon about your impending date and now you've got a face like a wet weekend.'

'I'm afraid I made a wee error when I ordered, Miss. I got distracted, you know, thinking about things.'

'Good grief, laddie,' said Munro as he unwrapped his sandwich, 'it's just a sausage toastie for goodness sake. What could possibly go wrong?'

'I asked for red sauce instead of brown.'

Munro rubbed his forehead and sighed heavily.

'Dougal,' he said, morosely. 'If I said to you "IC1," what would you say?'

Dougal, sensing a return trip to the café was on the cards, hesitated before answering.

'Caucasian male,' he said warily.

'Good. And if I said to you "SP70," what would you say?'

'Air support unit. Helicopter.'

'Good. And if I said "P45"?'

'Oh, leave him be,' said West, laughing as she finished her sandwich. 'Ignore him Dougal, he's winding you up.'

'Thank God for that, I never knew ordering the wrong sauce was a sackable offence. Anyone fancy a brew?'

'Not just yet,' said West, rubbing the crumbs from her fingers. 'Something we have to do first. Coming, Jimbo?'

'Where to?' said Munro.

'Downstairs. I'm going to charge MacAllister.'

'Aye, okay,' said Munro, reluctantly. 'If you're sure.'

Chapter 23

'And I thought it was only children who weren't supposed to play with knives,' said DCI Elliot as he raised his mug. 'I wish we had something a wee bit stronger to put in this, you've earned it, James.'

'It's not me you should be thanking, George,' said Munro as he stared out across the car park with his back to the group, 'it's Charlie. Oh, and Dougal, of course. All I did was lend some friendly advice, on sandwich fillings mainly. And the correct way to serve a steak.'

'Don't listen to him, Sir,' said West. 'He's too modest by far, if it wasn't for James…'

'Careful, Charlie, you're in danger of talking yourself out of a job!' said Elliot with a grin. 'I'll tell you this for nothing though, there's one person who is not best pleased with your efforts, the pair of you.'

'Really?' said West. 'Who's that, then?'

'The Fiscal. She's never been so busy. I'd give her a wide berth if I were you.'

'No need to worry on that score,' said Munro as he wandered to the desk and half-heartedly foraged through the sack containing Carducci's belongings. 'I'm away back home soon.'

'What do you mean "soon"?' said West. 'You can't do that. We're having dinner and drinks at mine tonight, even Dougal's coming, aren't you, Dougal?'

'I am indeed but I'm not staying late. I have to prepare for my weekend.'

'So, that's that then. You can leave in the morning and no arguments.'

'Aye, okay,' said Munro, as he fingered Carducci's wallet, telephone and keys, 'if we must.'

'Well, I'll see you all tonight,' said Elliot, as he turned for the door, 'and cheer up, James, no need to look so glum.'

'Maybe this'll cheer you up, Boss,' said Dougal, passing him a slip of paper.

'Och, Dougal man, I'm done here. What is this?'

'Telephone number for Miss McClure.'

'But we have her number.'

'It's her home number, Boss. She dropped by while you were downstairs, says you need to call her. I think she's under the impression that you and she are off to the cinema tonight.'

'Over my dead body,' said Munro, sneering as he tossed the paper in the bin. 'Over my dead body.'

'What's up, Jimbo?' said West, perturbed by his mood, 'something's riling you, I can tell. Can't be McClure, surely?'

'No, lassie, it's not McClure. Something's just not…'

'Well, maybe you should call her then. As a friend. You never know, she may be the key to whole new future.'

Munro stared at West, smiled wryly and winked.

'Grab your coat, Charlie,' he said as he tucked the sack under his arm, 'we've a few loose ends to tie up.'

Chapter 24

Despite the light but persistent rain and the occasional gust of wind blowing in off the fields, the front door – as was the way with many of the residents of Crosshill – was hanging ajar should friends or neighbours feel the urge to call in for a cup of tea and a chat, or to be more precise, to whinge about the cuts to the local bus service, the inadequate street lighting or the extortionate prices charged by the much maligned but life-savingly essential convenience store. Munro gently tapped the door and called inside.

'Hello?' he said, as he eased the door open. 'Anyone home? Mrs Buchanan?'

Heather Buchanan, beaming broadly, scuttled from the kitchen with a tea towel in one hand and an oven mitt in the other.

'Inspector!' she said excitedly, 'I thought I recognised the voice, and you too, Sergeant. My, this is a pleasant surprise, come in, come in and makes yourselves at home.'

'Thanking you,' said Munro, 'I hope we're not disturbing you, Heather, turning up like this, unannounced.'

'No, no, it's quite alright. Now, sit yourselves down. I'm just warming the pot and I've some scones fresh out of the oven. Shan't be a moment.'

West, looking more than a little confused, took a seat as Heather hastened to the kitchen and leaned into Munro.

'What the hell are we doing here?' she said, her voice no more than a whisper.

'All in good time, Charlie. All in good time.'

Heather returned bearing a tray laden with cups and saucers, a jug of milk, a teapot and a plate piled high with scones topped with clotted cream and strawberry jam.

'Now,' she said, 'you're not on parade so feel free to help yourself.'

'Very kind,' said Munro as West whipped one from the top of the pile and tucked in.

'So, to what do I owe the pleasure, Inspector?'

'Oh, it's just courtesy call, Heather. We wanted to check that you were okay…'

'Och, I'm fine, considering.'

'…and ask a couple of questions. Just to clarify a couple of things and to satisfy my own curiosity more than anything else.'

'Well ask away,' said Heather, 'I'll do my best to help.'

'Right you are,' said Munro, 'but first, I'm afraid I've some bad news for you. Your friend: Remo Carducci. I'm sorry to say he's passed on.'

Heather, cup poised halfway between the table and her mouth, stared at Munro.

'I'm not sure I understand, Inspector,' she said, 'I thought he'd gone to Italy. His father's birthday.'

'He didnae make it. It was quite… sudden.'

'I see. Oh dear. Dear, dear, dear. This is unexpected, quite the tragedy. Oh my, what about Anita? How will she…?'

'She's been informed, Heather, dinnae go worrying yourself about that now.'

'I must see her when she gets back, the poor woman, and so soon after Angus, too.'

'She'll not be back for a wee while,' said Munro, 'she's... extending her stay.'

'Can't say I blame her,' said Heather, taking a deep breath. 'Still, at least she's with family, that's always a comfort.'

'Aye, right enough. Listen, if you'd rather we came back another time...'

'No, no,' said Heather. 'You carry on, Inspector. It's fine. Really.'

Munro paused as West helped herself to another scone.

'Okay. Mr Carducci,' said Munro. 'Did you know that he owns a flat in Norway? It's in a place called Loddefjord?'

'Oh yes. He bought that years ago, in fact, not long after Lars joined the company.'

'Lars Gundersen?'

'Aye.'

'Good, I was coming to him,' said Munro. 'Would you happen to know why he bought the flat?'

'I do. I've not said anything before because Remo and Angus, God rest his soul, made it quite clear that I was not to meddle in their business.'

'Go on.'

'Lars's chosen line of work was not what you might call entirely... conventional.'

'In what way?' said West.

'He dealt in... organic tobacco, Sergeant.' said Heather, shaking her head. 'Och, it sounds terrible I know, but they said it was harmless. It was cannabis, I think. Remo and Angus met him on one of their golfing trips. After a few hours in the pub, he asked them if they'd be interested in taking some of his *merchandise* home with them.'

'Go on.'

'Well, Remo agreed of course and before long the cannabis was replaced with other... *things*. Lars rented the flat in Loddefjord, you see, and once the money came rolling in, Remo approached the owner and bought it so's they'd have somewhere secure to stay. Or to keep the drugs I imagine.'

'I'd never have guessed,' said West. 'Lovely scones by the way. But tell me, why did they get involved with this drugs thing in the first place? I mean, surely the restaurants...'

'Och, come, come, dear,' said Heather. 'Do you really think a café or two could make enough money to pay for his fancy motor car or all their golfing holidays?'

'No, I suppose not. But what about Angus? What was his role in all this?'

'He was canny,' said Heather. 'Clever. He knew how to move money around. Keep it out of sight, so to speak.'

'And that didn't bother you?' said West.

'What the eyes don't see, Sergeant, the heart doesn't feel.'

'So what happened to Lars, Heather?' said Munro. 'The last time we spoke you said he just vanished. That he stopped calling round.'

Heather settled back in her armchair, crossed her arms and smiled.

'We joked amongst ourselves, Inspector,' she said. 'Angus and I. We said Remo must have come from a long line of magicians because he was excellent at making folk disappear.'

'You mean...'

'That's exactly what I mean. I'm quite sure Lars wasn't the first. I can't prove it of course but if you asked me I'd say Remo wanted a bigger piece of the business and with Lars out of the way, he got it.'

'And when Lars disappeared and they were left without a driver, that's when you...'

'Brought Tommy over?' said Heather. 'Aye. Correct.'

'So you knew what he was doing?' said West. 'Tommy, I mean. You knew he was acting as some kind of courier?'

'All I knew, Sergeant, was that he'd been employed as a driver. Och, I had a fair idea of what he was up to, I'm not blind, but like I say, I can't prove any of it.'

Munro finished his tea, set his cup on the table and cleared his throat.

'Heather. Please understand I've no intention of upsetting you further so dinnae take offence but there's something I have to ask: you knew Angus was dead before we even found his body, didn't you? You knew it was Tommy who'd killed him?'

Heather nodded solemnly.

'I did,' she said. 'He telephoned me straight away. He told me everything.'

'And you didn't think to call the police?' said West. 'Surely that would have been…'

'And turn in my own brother, Sergeant? My own flesh and blood? I couldnae do it to him. I've told you before, he's not right in the head. He can't be held responsible for what he's done.'

'We realise that, Heather,' said Munro, 'and if it's any help, he'll be getting a full psychiatric assessment and we'll be in touch with the hospital in Oslo too. He'll be well looked after, I promise.'

'Good. That's a relief.'

'There's something else,' said Munro. 'Again, I apologise in advance for asking it but… Angus and Anita.'

Heather allowed herself a wry smirk.

'Angus and Anita,' she said. 'That's been going on for years. The old fool thought I didnae have a clue. Silly bugger.'

'But you let them get away with it?' said West. 'Right under your nose?'

'What else was I to do, dear?' said Heather. 'If I'd said anything at all he'd have either denied it or pleaded for forgiveness and I'm far too old to put up with such spineless behaviour.'

'Fair enough.'

'Incidentally,' said Heather, tapping the side of her nose. 'I've some news for you, too. Did you know that Remo was cheating too? He was having an affair with that manageress up in Prestwick.'

'Aye,' said Munro. 'We knew about that.'

'You did? Och, well, I was only trying to help.'

'Well, I think we've taken up enough of your time, Heather, you've been most helpful.'

'Nae bother, Inspector. You're always welcome here.'

'Very kind, I'm sure. Oh, there is just one more thing.'

'Go on.'

'Your keys,' said Munro. 'The Carducci's kept a spare set at their place, we know that because that's how we got you back in.'

'That's right,' said Heather, 'I still feel foolish about that, such a bother over nothing.'

'I was wondering, do you keep a spare set for them?'

'I do indeed. I keep them on my chain. I can't recall the number of times they've woken us up at one in the morning, much the worse for wear, I might add but I'm not complaining, that's just the way it is.'

'Of course,' said Munro, 'after all, what are friends for?'

'Exactly.'

'But here's the thing, Heather. See, I dinnae think you locked yourself out of your own home that morning.'

'I'm not sure I follow, Inspector.'

'And I dinnae think you raced over to see Remo to fetch the spare set.'

'I don't understand.'

'I think,' said Munro as he retrieved a clear plastic bag from his coat pocket, 'I think you locked yourself out of the Carducci residence.'

Munro opened the bag and pulled out a set of keys as West, almost choking on her scone, turned to face him and slowly smiled.

'We found these hanging from the lock on the inside of Carducci's front door. I couldnae figure it out at first, I mean, why would the Carducci's have a key fob with the letter "B" on it. Then I realised, these dinnae belong to them at all, do they? They belong to you. Am I right?'

Heather, saying nothing, simply nodded.

'See,' continued Munro, 'I think you went to Carducci's place that morning and let yourself in. I think you found him sitting peacefully in his armchair, listening to his headphones while he worked off a hangover. And you took your chance. You took the knife from the kitchen and you stabbed him through the neck.'

Munro walked to window, stood with hands clasped behind his back and stared out across the fields.

'See, Heather,' he said, 'I understand how much you loved Angus, despite his failings. I know you tolerated his behaviour just to keep him by your side but when Tommy called you and told you what he'd done, you knew Remo was behind it.'

'Aye, I did,' said Heather softly. 'As soon as Tommy mentioned that MacAllister woman, I knew Remo was to blame. I knew it was him. An eye for an eye, Inspector. He robbed me of my Angus. I could see no good reason why he should be the one to enjoy the spoils of their efforts.'

Munro turned to face Heather and caught her eye, hesitating before he spoke.

'Did you know Angus and Anita were planning to run away together? To Loddefjord?'

'No. I did not.'

'Angus was on his way there, to the ferry terminal, when it happened. Anita was going to join him later.'

'Is that so?' said Heather, huffing with disgust. 'Well in that case, maybe he got what he deserved, Inspector. Maybe he got what he deserved, after all.'

* * *

'You knew all along, didn't you?' said West as they watched Heather ease herself into the back of a patrol car. 'You knew it was Heather who'd killed Carducci.'

'No, Charlie. I didn't,' said Munro. 'All I knew was, it wasnae MacAllister.'

'But how? I mean, all the evidence was stacked against her. Everything. How the hell could you doubt it?'

'Instinct, lassie. Now, let's get you back to the office, you've a heap of paperwork to get through before your guests arrive and I need an early night. Tomorrow I'll be sleeping in my own bed.'

Epilogue

West – normally self-assured and more than capable of fighting her own corner despite the occasional pangs of self-doubt – parked the Figaro, glanced up at the office on the third floor and, overwhelmed by an irrational sense of nervous trepidation, slumped back in her seat and sighed. With no Munro to back her up, she sought a degree of reassurance from her phone, optimistically checking for any missed calls or messages wishing her luck before, somewhat disappointedly, heading inside.

'Dougal!' she said, forcing a smile, 'first in, as usual, I see.'

'Morning, Miss. How's tricks?'

'Yeah, all good. How about you? Did you enjoy your fishing date?'

Dougal hesitated.

'Aye, it was okay,' he said. 'Actually, no. It was a complete disaster.'

'Why? Did it not go according to plan?'

'I didnae have a plan, Miss. But Lizzie did. I should've listened to the boss. She wasnae interested in fishing at all, all she wanted to do was…'

'I get the picture,' said West, smirking. 'Is that why you look so down?'

'No, no,' said Dougal, 'I can live without Lizzie, it's the case I cannae figure. I mean, what makes an old lady like Heather Buchanan do something like that? Just stab someone in the neck?'

West sat down and propped her feet on the desk.

'Resentment, Dougal,' she said. 'Years of resentment.'

'I still don't get it.'

'I do,' said West, 'I get it totally. You see, Heather devoted her life to Angus, right? She was his wife, his best friend, his housekeeper, his cook, his everything. She did her best by him and she was proud of it too, but all he did in return, was betray her. Then her best friend betrayed her. And then her best friend's husband betrayed her. I guess she just got fed up with being taken for a mug, knowing what was going on right under her nose, bottling it all up and letting them get away with it.'

'So, she just snapped?' said Dougal.

'Yeah, if you like. I don't blame her, either. If it was up to me I'd let her off.'

'Well, she nearly got away with it.'

'Yeah, thanks for reminding me about that, Dougal. Nice one.'

'I didnae mean it like that, Miss. You did a brilliant job. I mean, all the evidence pointed to MacAllister. Even a jury would've sent her down.'

'Maybe.'

'So how did you figure out it was Buchanan?' said Dougal.

'Instinct.'

'Instinct?'

'Something Jimbo said.'

'Okay,' said Dougal. 'And how is he, by the way? Back home, now?'

'Yup,' said West, ruefully. 'Back home and probably half way up a mountain or knee-deep in compost, as we speak.'

* * *

Though not an ardent traveller, of the handful of hotels, guest houses and coaching inns Munro had had the sometimes-dubious pleasure of experiencing, those which held the fondest memories were the ones which reminded him of home. Despite the clinical surroundings of his room in the Dumfries Royal Infirmary, however – its stark, white walls and grating overhead light being the complete antithesis of what he deemed "comfortable" – he lay with his head propped up on two firm pillows, wallowing in the soundest sleep he'd enjoyed in years, oblivious to the rhythmic beep of the heart monitor by his side and the two figures hovering over his bed.

'I came as quick as I could,' said DCI Elliot. 'Can he hear us?'

Doctor McKay, his voice soft and low, spoke candidly.

'Possibly,' he said, 'but there's no real way of knowing, not with concussion. The man's taken a quite a wallop – three cracked ribs, a fractured clavicle and a broken arm, not to mention the bruising. What he needs is complete rest, he'll come round in time.'

'You're sure of that? I mean, he's not going to…'

'No, no, he'll make a full recovery, Inspector. I'm positive.'

'Thank God for that.'

'Has he any next of kin?' said McKay. 'He's going to need some looking-after once he's up and about.'

'No, no-one to speak of, Doctor,' said Elliot, 'not since his wife passed away. I suppose Charlie's the nearest he's got to family now.'

'And that would be his nephew? Or a cousin, perhaps?'

'No, no. Charlie's like the daughter he never had. She'll be here in an hour or two.'

'Good. We should leave him be now, give him some peace. There's a couple of gentlemen outside I'm sure you're keen to talk to, that'll take your mind off it.'

'Right enough, Doctor. You'll let me know of any change, won't you? Especially if he wakes up?'

'You'll be the first to know, Inspector. I guarantee it.'

* * *

The two officers, dwarfed by Elliot's towering frame, leapt to their feet like a couple of schoolkids about to receive a grilling from the headmaster.

'DC Duncan Reid, Sir,' said the one in plain clothes. 'And this is PC Ferguson.'

Elliot, bemoaning the fact that neither looked capable of winning a pub quiz let alone conducting an investigation, eyed them sceptically and sighed.

'Okay, lads,' he said, 'let's have it.'

'He was in Dalbeattie, Sir,' said Reid, 'by all accounts, stocking up on groceries.'

'Aye, that figures,' said Elliot, 'he's been with me up in Ayr the past week.'

'He'd made a couple of trips to the shops already, there were bags in the boot of his car from the supermarket and the butcher. According to witnesses, he'd just dropped a third bag in the back and was walking around to the driver's side door when he was hit.'

'Hit?'

'Aye. It seems the car came straight at him. A deliberate hit and run.'

'You're sure?' said Elliot. 'There's no chance he could've stepped out without looking? Or that the driver was distracted, on his phone, maybe?'

'No, no,' said Reid, 'the car came at speed, he was doing at least forty, swerved right into him and took off down the High Street. If you asked me, I'd say it's probably someone with a grudge.'

'Is that so?' said Elliot sarcastically.

'Aye. Does DI Munro have any enemies, Sir?'

'Put it this way, laddie. He doesn't have many friends. What about the car?'

'A white VW Golf, Sir,' said Ferguson, flipping open his notebook. 'A two door, GTI which now has damage to the nearside headlamp and wing mirror. We're still trying to trace it but so far...'

'Did you get the number?'

'We did, Sir. It was registered as SORN to an address in Prestwick almost three years ago so it's been off the road a wee while. All we have is the last registered keeper of the vehicle, so not much use.'

'Probably stolen, then,' said Elliot. 'And you've checked it's not been returned to that address?'

'We have. No sign of it.'

'Okay,' said Elliot. 'Just out of interest, who was the last registered keeper?'

'Let me see,' said Ferguson, flicking through his notebook. 'It was owned by a fella called Gundersen, Sir.'

Elliot froze, his eyes narrowing as he scowled at the officers.

'Gundersen?' he said.

'Aye, Lars Gundersen. But apparently he's no longer at that address.'

'Who is?'

Ferguson hesitated as ran through his notes.

'A lady called MacAllister, Sir. Miss Clare MacAllister.'

'Are you okay, Sir?' said Reid nervously. 'Rest assured, I'll do everything I can to make sure we get this fella. I guarantee it.'

'You'll do no such thing, laddie,' said Elliot, reaching for his phone as he stormed off down the corridor. 'From now on, you'll be working under Detective Sergeant Charlotte West. Do I make myself clear?'

Character List

DI JAMES MUNRO – Shrewd, smart and cynical with an inability to embrace retirement, he has a knack for expecting the unexpected.

DS CHARLOTTE WEST – Finally overcoming her self-doubt after a floundering engagement, she finds her feet and regains her confidence with Munro as her mentor in his native Scotland.

DC DOUGAL McCRAE – A clever, young and unintentionally single introvert with more brain than brawn who'd rather be fishing than drinking in the pub.

DCI GEORGE ELLIOT – Laid back and relaxed, happy behind a desk and happiest at home, he prefers to let others do the dirty work having spent a lifetime dicing with death.

REMO CARDUCCI – Proud of his Italian heritage and his buxom wife, Remo is an ostentatious narcissist with an eye for the ladies, fast cars and designer clothes who spends his time overseeing his chain of restaurants.

ANITA CARDUCCI – Married to Remo, she considers herself to be the epitome of Italian style and runs her own hair salon more as a hobby than a business.

ANGUS BUCHANAN – A retired, easy going and affable bon-viveur, Angus – lifelong friend and business partner of Remo – manages the restaurants' finances as well as his wife's.

HEATHER BUCHANAN – Independent, industrious and at her happiest when looking after other people, Heather prides herself on her skills as a housewife and, despite her ability to render anything she puts in the oven inedible, as a cook.

TOMEK DUBROWSKI – Scarred by a troubled upbringing as a result of his low IQ and regarded as unsociable, unemployable and untrustworthy, Tomek, in spite of his differences, has an insatiable urge to please everyone he meets.

CLARE MacALLISTER – Brash, single and lonely with an over-inflated ego and a desperate need to feel loved, she'll take her chances with anybody.

MISS MARGARET McCLURE – Mature, professional and bored of dining alone, she craves companionship and thinks she's found her future partner in the single but unattainable DI Munro.

If you enjoyed this book, please let others know by leaving a quick review on Amazon. Also, if you spot anything untoward in the paperback, get in touch. We strive for the best quality and appreciate reader feedback.

editor@thebookfolks.com

www.thebookfolks.com

ALSO BY PETE BRASSETT

In this series:

SHE – book 1
AVARICE – book 2
ENMITY – book 3
TERMINUS – book 5
TALION – book 6

Other titles:

THE WILDER SIDE OF CHAOS
YELLOW MAN
CLAM CHOWDER AT LAFAYETTE AND SPRING
THE GIRL FROM KILKENNY
BROWN BREAD
PRAYER FOR THE DYING
KISS THE GIRLS

Printed in Great Britain
by Amazon